MW01137154

# Six Bits

By

# Laurence E Dahners

Copyright 2015
Laurence E Dahners
Kindle Edition

# Table of Contents

SANDER ...............................................3
EXCELTOR ......................................27
MACOS...............................................94
PORTER..........................................120
BILLY BENOIT..............................166
GUITAR GIRL.................................204
The End ..........................................216
Acknowledgements.......................217

## SANDER

On this, the 25th anniversary of the establishment of
Sander's School for Underprivileged Children, it is my
intention to make public the true story of why and how
the school came to be established and named.
The story you've been told is not true. I wasn't really
the one who first saw the alien ship. It was instead the
namesake of this school, a fellow known to my family
as Sander. No doubt you know of him by a different
and ill-regarded name, but I wish to shine a kinder
light on this troubled man's soul.
I was twelve years old when my family first hired
Sander. My dad had been using the net to search for
a hired hand for a couple of months and there hadn't
been a flicker of interest to that point.

By then my folks had been working a $10^{13}$ kilogram
nickel iron 'roid for about ten years. Course nickel and
iron wasn't worth much out in the asteroid belt but this
'roid had a surprisingly high content of rhenium.
Rhenium, you'll remember, was in high demand at
that time for the production of high-strength, high-
temperature ReTiCuO superconductors.
We were pretty isolated out there. Living inside that
small mountain of ore as it slowly roamed the hard
black void of space, we kept in touch with other
belters by laser or radio, but seldom breathed the
same air as other human beings. Our social calendar
was mostly determined by the 'roid's elliptical orbit. It
swung in pretty far, coming nearly as close to the sun
as the Earth. When I was eight, Terra was in our part
of her orbit during our close swing and we actually ran
an orbital transfer over to Earth with the boat and
delivered some product in person. We gawked, acted
like tourists and generally saw mankind's birthplace.

3

We only stayed three weeks, but the kids I lasered with out in the belt quizzed me for days on what it was like. They especially wanted to know what it felt like to be in a crowd. We sometimes visited belt communities on big 'roids when we got close to them, but that wasn't often and those outposts of civilization were all pretty small.

My Dad worked pretty hard mining the "Rock," as we called our 'roid. He did it with a fusion-powered torch. He was big, like I am now, angular, gruff and hard working. When I was caught up with the school computer, I'd sometimes go with him to sit in his cabin on the torch while he was blasting away at the parts of the Rock that appeared promising. He hunched over his screens with intense concentration. The torch was essentially a big set of superconducting magnets that controlled a hot fusion containment field. The miniature sun thus produced blew out one side of the containment and heated rock to a vapor which was sucked up and separated. Good stuff like rhenium was condensed out in collectors and stored for delivery in the raw state. The "slag," as we called it, was pumped out to Mom.

Mom's control room was entirely different from Dad's. Where his was utilitarian and plain, she decorated hers. She had a couple of big wallscreens devoted to constantly displaying things of beauty. Sometimes it would be art, other times scenes from Earth or Saturn.

Mom used the slag, which was mostly nickel-iron, to make "product." Apparently she had a real talent for it, 'cause she was always getting offers to move to one of the belt communities where she'd be closer to the demand. Essentially what she did was inject alloying materials, then gas into Dad's molten slag to make a foam out of the nickel-iron. Then she blew it into various useful shapes in the microgravity. Using various techniques, she could make the foam denser in certain parts of a structure and heavily alloy areas where she needed more strength. After that she'd add layers of solid material to reinforce high stress areas. You might think that production of stuff like that could be handled entirely by computer, and you'd be mostly right nowadays, but back then it was still an art that was well beyond a machine's intelligence. The production of anything at all complex required true virtuosity like my mother's. For the most part she was making large, very-low mass structures with tremendous mechanical strength. Good stuff for boats, since they need high strength, but can't afford to mass much or it takes too long to accelerate 'em. I guess there was a lot of demand on Earth too 'cause of gravity, but fabbers in LEO made most of that stuff. Even so, when Mom didn't have belt orders to fill, she made stuff for Earth on standing orders. The feeling I got was that she was so good at it that they were always happy to have her product if they could get it. Not happy enough, however, to pay the transport margin over the prices she could get in the belt. Anyway we were needin' some help. Even though I was gettin' old enough to be some help, I wasn't much good 'cause I hadn't gotten far enough in school yet. I could handle a 'puter, but I was still pretty slow. Besides, I had to spend most of my time with the school 'puter.

Actually, I think I could interface pretty well for a kid, but Dad was never satisfied. It being his theory that self-satisfaction was the enemy of personal improvement, sometimes he'd sit down and show me just how much faster he was.

Mom, on the other hand, believed in encouragement. She always praised me for what I *could* do. She was small. Even at twelve I was bigger than she was, and by my memory, she was really pretty; short blond hair, bouncy, fun, full of energy. She'd tell me how proud she was of me, but hell, she could beat Dad at almost any 'puter task, so praise from her, when he was so critical, kinda gave me whiplash.

My sister Gen was about 9 then and, to the great distress of me her older sibling, was a faster interfacer than I'd been when I was 9. She didn't let me forget how good she was for her age and I worried that she'd surpass me.

'Puters weren't as independent back then as they are now. Course they could do a lot on their own, but they really needed a human to provide direction for anything but rote tasks. Dad, bein' a pretty good interfacer, could run the 'puter on the torch and the one on the vapor separator and several smaller ones that kept the mining operation going, pretty much all at the same time. Mom ran five to ten at a time to make her production runs. Course she couldn't run that many constantly 'cause it took such intense concentration. She only did it for a few minutes at a time during the actual foaming. She ran just 2 to 5 most of the rest of the time when she was trimming, stressing, and melding various pieces.

My most important chore was to keep an eye on the household 'puter. For those of you that live on a planet, that may not sound like much, but you've got to remember that our household consisted of some air filled tunnels on the Rock. Household mistakes could leave us without air, water, or food. Believe me, if we'd had to pack up the boat and leave the rock to purchase some life-essential at a time when there wasn't a good transfer orbit, my ass would have been in the proverbial sling with my dad.

So an extra adult would have made things a lot more efficient. Mom and Dad spent a lot of time helping each other with tasks that required two interfacers and the interruptions hurt both of their efficiencies. Besides with all the equipment they had, it only made sense to work the machines more hours a day. Our capital investment was wasted while Mom and Dad were sleeping.

So we'd been 'netting for about a month, looking for someone short on capital. Someone who'd be willing to work for a wage. However, belters tended not to be the types who wanted to work for someone else, so we hadn't been having much luck.

Apparently, nobody was really broke right then.

One day when I interfaced with the household 'puter it became obvious that we were about to have a visitor. The passive sensors had picked up a boat that was decelerating at a rate to park it in our orbit. This was a scary thing because people didn't usually transfer into someone's orbit without calling ahead. There were plenty of pirates around back then, so that's the first panicked thought that came to our minds. On the other hand we didn't make a great target for a pirate except when our rhenium stores were high and we'd recently off-loaded, so we were puzzled why a pirate would choose to come right then. Our sensors were pretty good, so we'd picked him up about 36 hours out. I told Mom and Dad what was going on and soon we were all worrying and following the plan dad had established in case this ever happened.

We set up our laser to transmit an auto-message to Ceres base at the first sign of trouble. Then we set up the outside 'bots that normally did Mom's work so that they could be controlled from the cabin of our own boat. All the food was harvested out of our greenhouse and we stocked the boat with even more water and air. We normally kept it stocked for 10 days more than what we calculated for a fast transfer orbit to the nearest belt community. All our valuables and refined rhenium were moved into a deep tunnel and Mom sealed it off. We all moved into the boat 30 minutes before the newcomer matched orbits and Mom resumed trimming operations from an interface in the boat to make it look like we were just doing business as usual. Dad had interfaced with the three big industrial lasers and aimed them at the visitor's approximate arrival point, then hid them behind thin sheets of slag. I 'faced with one of the small lasers and Gen with the other.

It was kind of an anticlimax when the newcomer came to a perfect match, cut his thruster without a single correcting push and hit us dead center with a tight beam message laser on low power. "Name's Sander. I'm answering your ad on the net. Still got a job open?"

"Why didn't you message ahead?"

"Didn't think you'd have any takers."

We discussed it a while and decided he couldn't be a pirate. He was there in a singleship that didn't have much freight acceleration capability. Not that it didn't have the thrusters for it, you understand, but it didn't have the kind of structure you'd need to attach freight. It was the kind of boat small prospectors favored for drifting around the belt, searching for a high grade 'roid. *Not* what you'd use for harvesting a 'roid. *Certainly* not what you'd use if you were a pirate. It had a big thruster at one end of a cylindrical life support module. Some attitude jets at the other end. Reflective surfaces so you could be easily found if you got in trouble.

Of course this "drifter's boat" suggested that he might not be the kind of upstanding character that we'd like, but Mom and Dad had talked about who they might get before they advertised and this was exactly the kind of fellow who they'd thought might need this kind of job. A down-on-his-luck, unsociable, loner type, so to speak.

So we took him on.

Sander was a small fellow, maybe thirty or thirty-five. What was left of his hair was cut really short. Slender but wiry, he was given to small precise movements.

He claimed to have been born on Earth which may have explained his small stature, but he sure handled himself well in microgravity. He hardly ever spoke unless spoken to, and then he spoke slowly, usually after a pause to ponder.

When you talked to him you'd almost think he wasn't too bright. You'd never think that after you'd seen him 'faced with a 'puter though. Even back then it was pretty commonly accepted that high intelligence was necessary to interface well, though you could be plenty smart and still not be able to 'face. Believe me though, when *Sander* was 'faced, the 'puters and their 'bots performed flawlessly.

You can imagine what happened. Me a lonely 12 year old; not much personal contact with other people; suddenly confronted with a quiet unassuming fellow who could perform miracles with 'puters and 'bots. I got a bad case of hero worship.

In my book, one of his most amazing feats was the ability to set himself spinning in space with such a perfect twist that he could do several hundred revolutions without drifting far enough to bump into anything. He claimed it put his mind at rest like yoga (whatever that is). The few times I tried it, it made me want to barf.

Sander brewed a serious microgravity beer. Had a little spinner-vat and special yeast. He'd spend hours tinkering with "The System" as he called it. Dad said it was the finest beer he'd ever had.

Best was just watching him work the 'bots with one of the 'puters. They would work in perfect unison performing tasks so smoothly that it was like a ballet. You'd never see a 'bot he was controlling in standby, waiting for its portion of a task to come up. No, it would be doing something useful while waiting. It seemed to be a point of pride with him. Once when he had a 'bot doing an intermittent task that had a measly thirty second wait period during which it really couldn't accomplish anything else useful, he had the 'bot spin during the breaks. The 'bot would spin free, then suddenly break spin, perform its task and spin up again. He'd only done it a few times though, when a laser came sailing over, apparently pitched by one of the other 'bots while I wasn't paying attention. The previously spinning 'bot started using that laser to punch holes that were needed in a piece of work across the room. It'd task, pivot, fire the laser a few times and then turn back to its original task. I hated to even think about the kind of control it would take to have a 'bot perform close tolerance laser punches from across the room like that.

The guy was so talented that I wasn't surprised to hear Mom and Dad talking about him one night, almost as if they were suspicious. Dad was saying, "I don't know why a guy as talented as he is would need to take a job with us. He could get a better paying job anywhere from low Earth orbit to Ganymede."

There was a little silence, then Mom said slowly, "I don't know. He seems kinda sad. As if something *terrible* happened in his life. I asked him once, but he said he didn't want to talk about it… He didn't deny something bad happening though. Maybe his wife or even his whole family died or something like that? Maybe he's just looking for a quiet place to recover."

Sander'd been with us about two, maybe three months when the other 'roid happened by. Now I know *everyone* has already heard all about that other 'roid, but I've got to tell the story my way.

We first picked it up with our collision screens. Not that it was going to collide, which is an incredibly rare event in the belt, but our screen had been set up to warn us of anything even coming close. We'd been hoping to find a carbonaceous chunk of rock which might provide us with some of the raw material for Mom's alloys. They were costing a fortune to import and she was having to avoid certain kinds of jobs because the price of alloying ingredients kept her from being cost competitive. So we analyzed images of this one and decided it must be carbonaceous from its low albedo. We hadn't had much hope of finding such a thing since they're usually farther out, but there're a lot of freaky orbits in the belt.

A lot of talk ensued, weighing the pros and cons of trying to warp part of it into *our* orbit. The obvious thing was for Sander to take our boat over to it, blow it apart and bring in the most appropriate chunk. That way Mom and Dad could pretty much keep on schedule. Some of it might take an extra hand, but I could go along and help. This led to some heated discussions between my parents about whether I was old enough, whether Sander could be trusted with me, whether Sander could be trusted with the boat and so on.

I pointed out that my folks would still have Sander's boat and he'd been trustworthy so far. After *way* too much discussion, to my delight he and I loaded up and started out.

On the way over we talked about orbital mechanics. He taught me a lot by taking me through those calculations. How long it would take to accelerate how big a chunk of the 'roid sufficiently to match its orbit to the Rock. It already matched our orbit fairly well or it would have been impossible to take any more than a small chunk. Mom and Dad had decided that we could spend up to two weeks pushing on our selected piece. We ran some trial solutions on the 'puter and decided that if it massed more than $5 \times 10^5$ kilograms, establishing a transfer orbit would take too long. We also discussed how we might place our charge in the hopes of blowing a chunk *bigger* than $5 \times 10^5$ in the right direction so that we'd be able to move it with less push.

Those were glory days for me since my hero worship of Sander was in full flower. Havin' him spend all that time talkin' to me really made me feel important, even though I knew deep inside that he really didn't have anything better to do.

I got the feeling he *liked* talking to me and felt quite proud of it.

When we got to the 'roid, we nudged up against it, gave it a push, read our accelerometers, and calculated its mass at $4\times10^{10}$ kilos. It was mostly black indicating a lot of carbon and its low density suggested the same. It was really rough and irregular and didn't have much spin. It shouldn't be too hard to break a few big chunks off it with properly placed charges. Sander pointed out that the deeper we were inside it when we started lasering the holes for the charges, the less time it would take to place deep charges. So we took a pass around it looking for a crack of some kind we could get down into. We found a crevice on the far side big enough to drive the boat into, which we did.

Of course, you know that's where we found the alien craft.

I didn't know what the hell was goin' on at first. Just that Sander had stopped us cold and was hangin' there in his acceleration web with a blank look on his face. So I looked where he was lookin'.

There on one roughhewn black face of the crevice, fixed in the center of the sharply outlined area lit by our work lights, I saw the aliens' boat. Now, you know it didn't look much like one of the little craft that traveled the belt. I don't even think I recognized it as a boat right away.

But I could tell it was something manufactured.

It didn't take long for me to figure out it hadn't been made by humans.

By its streamlined shape you could tell that it was meant for atmospheric flight. On that basis alone you knew it wasn't human. No reason to have streamlined shapes out in the belt; ergo there wasn't anything human *and* streamlined in the belt.

I remember the sweat breakin' out on my forehead and the ringing in my ears. My own voice sounded real distant as it trailed off on whatever trivial question I had been jabberin' about at the time.

To some extent, I was filled with wonder and awe over the secrets that might be held by such an artifact. Partly I was considering the possibility that there might be live aliens aboard training some kind of "blaster" on us, though even at that moment, I think I knew that the artifact had been long abandoned, maybe even hundreds of millennia ago.

Mostly, though, I was terrified of Sander. Even though I'd been worshiping the air he hung in a minute ago, my mind had already snapped around 180° with the awful and certain realization of what this kind of discovery could do to a man. At that time, you may know, anything you found in the belt was your exclusive property unless someone could prove that they had visited it first, marked it, and laid claim to it at Ceres. It was the kind of discovery that could have had *brothers* at each other's throats, much less a man and a kid he barely knew.

If you found it while working for someone else it belonged to them.

My sphincters were twitching. I knew *immediately* that I was the only thing that stood between Sander and unimaginable wealth, or at least probable wealth assuming that even a *few* technical secrets were hidden in yon artifact! Space me, move the alien boat, blow up the 'roid.

Come back with a sad story about how I got caught in the explosion somehow.

Then all he'd have to do is quit his job, wait a while, then come back and "find" the artifact. He'd be rich beyond anyone's dreams.

I could hear the blood roaring in my ears and I'd been staring at Sander with eyes that hadn't blinked for a minute when he slowly turned to me. "Well kid," he said. "It looks like you and your folks have really struck it big this time."

I wanted to believe him. Make that, "I did believe him." Yet somehow I couldn't.

For the next six hours, while we were detaching that thing from the 'roid and loading it onto the freight boom of our boat, my heart shot up and down my throat in irregular cycles. We didn't want to damage the alien ship, but it was firmly anchored to the 'roid. We finally used some small torches to cut the rock away from the anchor points rather than cut the anchors. Seems kind of silly now, the discussion we had about whether or not to cut the anchors. Course, at the time, we had no way of knowing that there wasn't a tool in the solar system that *would* cut those damn anchors!

Anyway, we were having trouble cutting the rock away with the 'bots and so Sander suggested that we suit up and "get a closer look." A couple of dozen scenarios involving torches "accidentally" cuttin' me in half went through my mind, but I managed to follow him out there and sure enough, with the additional perspective that being there gives you, we had the alien boat loose in no time.

From pictures of the alien boat, you know that it was kind of a flattened ovoid with a fin toward one end and anchor points on the underside. There weren't any kind of regular attachment points of course. We had to use cable to lash it to the freight boom.

Then believe it or not we drilled and blew the 'roid. It seems silly in retrospect, but we figured the alien boat might not pan out and there may never be another carbonaceous 'roid this close. We picked out a likely $3 \times 10^4$ kg fragment already travelling somewhat our way, attached to it, stopped its rotation and started accelerating it into a transfer orbit to the Rock.

We looked the artifact over with 'bots, but of course didn't suit up and look at it in person while under acceleration. We lost one 'bot for the duration of the trip by sending it into the alien airlock. That's how we figured out that we couldn't communicate with a 'bot through the walls of the artifact.

During that time all my dreams were nightmares. Sometimes about slimy aliens, but usually in those dreams I had Sander chasing me on, and on, and on... He'd be accompanied by a couple of 'bots with lasers and I wouldn't feel like I had a chance in hell.

I wanted to radio ahead to tell my folks what we'd found, but Sander said we needed to keep radio silence about the artifact. That made me even more uneasy.

To my amazement, I was still in one piece when we arrived back at the Rock. At first I was moved to worship again by Sander's selflessness, but shortly thereafter started worrying about what he might do to my whole family.

Well when my folks saw the artifact, I got to see them go through the same kind of awe/wonder/fear/panic thing I'd gone through a few days before. Their approach to it was to immediately offer Sander a quarter share in any profits. The profits looked to be astronomical anyway so it seemed a smart thing to do.

Then they did the stupid thing.

They filed a "description of claim" with Ceres by laser. Figured that with the claim published and Sander staked to a quarter, he'd be crazy to backstab us. He'd never be able to turn in an individual claim if something bad happened to all of us. There'd be a hell of an inquiry.

I was heading to my room that night when I heard them talking. Sander said, "You filed a claim with *Ceres*?!"

My mother said, "Yes! With the claim published in all of our names, we don't have to worry about…" here, she probably realized she was about to say, *you jumping the claim,* so she stumbled a little, "um, someone trying to jump the claim."

"My God!" Sander said, as if he couldn't believe his ears. "You don't know… no, I guess you don't," he said sadly.

"Don't know what."

"The claims office at Ceres, it leaks like a sieve. There are people there who probably called their pirate contacts before they even finished filing your claim," he said, sounding kind of sad.

As expected, we were receiving almost constant laser traffic within six hours of the filing. It took a while for word to get around the solar system, even at the speed of light, but there are a *lot* of programs out there that search message traffic for things that might be of financial/technical/scientific use and they ALL came down on an alien artifact. We were working with our lawyer, sorting offers. Let me tell you *he* was one happy son.

In all the excitement, I slacked my chores and so it was 36 hours before I checked the household 'puter and found out we had an unannounced visitor *burning* in, due in 18 hours! Whoever it was, they were pulling high Gs.

We back figured their orbit to try to find out where they were from. They hadn't originated from any of the known belt communities. We searched our incoming message traffic and *no one* had contacted us to say they were coming.

Even before we did that, there wasn't much hope. That inbound boat had to be pirates.

Sander took the news with a look of grim resignation on his face. He didn't say, "I told you so," though he certainly could have. In retrospect, it's pretty obvious that he *knew* what kind of trouble the claim submission would bring us.

My parents tried to send me away while they talked about what to do, but I raised hell until they finally gave in and let me listen. An obvious strategy would have been to hide the alien boat, but it was too big to fit into any of our existing tunnels. We couldn't enlarge one enough in the time we had. Looked like we had two choices: One, hide ourselves and let them take the artifact. Two, stay out and fight.

If we chose the first, we could try to trace the pirates and hope we could convince one of the belt communities to help us go out and take the artifact back. Theoretically, the pirates would be easy to trace because they couldn't change direction without using their thrusters and thrusters generate a megahertz signal that's easy to track. In reality they could match with a small 'roid and attach to it with a cable. Then they'd use thrusters to build up angular acceleration around the rock. After turning off the thrusters they could release the cable and fly off going any direction. If they coasted for a few weeks before they fired up their thrusters again, nobody'd know it was them. Besides, most of the belt communities weren't going to go chasing pirates on our behalf.

Option two wasn't very appealing either. We had two mining torches and the construction lasers that made pretty good weapons, but we were going to be working against some people who presumably really *did* know how to fight, had real armaments and only had to make us keep our heads down until they'd applied boost to the artifact.

You know the saying about, "Either go in with your head up and fight like hell (if you think you can win) or put your tail between your legs and run like hell (if you think you'll lose)."

Of course, we decided on a crappy combination of the two.

Dad enlarged the mouth of one of our tunnels. We laid the alien boat into it and Mom covered it with some foam steel. Then she put on a layer of slag that kind of looked like the surface of the Rock and was supposed to act as camouflage. That took her most of the 18 hours.

Dad set us up down in a deep tunnel. He set up hard wired connections to the surface so we could remote control our "weapons" from down in our hidey hole. Sander generally helped out everywhere. I remember thinking that his suggestions for laser placement were downright scary 'cause they suggested he'd been through this kinda stuff before.

We'd generally agreed that the artifact wasn't worth losing a life over so we were going to fight a remote battle even though we wouldn't have very good control. We sent out messages to the belt communities asking for help and got a few "wish we coulds." This was even when we promised big money from the artifact for help. No one thought we had any chance in hell of keeping it, so to them it would be a bleak investment.

When zero hour arrived, we all clambered down into our hide, deep inside the 'roid and got ready to man our "battle stations" on the remotes. Sander ran up to his room at the last minute to "get something he'd forgotten".

I was worried about my hero and so I monitored his room sensor to be sure he got there and started back in time. On the monitor he arrived, pulled a flat case out of his locker, opened it and pulled out a vest. When he put it on I recognized it as a "power jacket" by the flat 'puter compartments on the front and the single large disk of a fusion generator on the back. A generator like that was probably capable of producing something like 10-20 megawatts. He hooked up its output leads to the front compartments and then pulled out a ring interfacer. He slipped the ring onto the back of his head and plugged it into the front compartments of the jacket. I'd never seen a skull ring interfacer before, but knew what it was right away. Invented by an evil genius pirate known only as "the Sandman," a ring interfacer allowed 'puter interface by brain wave monitoring, and required intense concentration to control superfluous wave formation. Everyone dreamed of being able to use them, but supposedly only 20 to 30 people had ever proved to have that kind of control. Even most of them could only do it as kind of a party trick, not as something really effective.

Dad musta heard me suck in my breath 'cause I heard him start swearing softly. I turned and saw him staring at my screen.

Sander pulled out a final piece of equipment and headed for the lock. He grabbed his suit, snapped out the standard HUD (Heads Up Display) and put in the one he'd just brought from his room. He was in that suit and out the lock faster than anyone I've ever seen suit up, before or since.

Sure enough 30 seconds later not a single one of our remotes controlled a thing. I'd seen power jackets before and seen people run equipment with them. I'd even heard of people with enough computer and broadcast power to take over other peoples 'bots. It was supposedly a favorite pirate trick—especially the Sandman's—to turn your own equipment against you, but it's supposed to take time and hypothetically it's impossible against hardwired equipment. We'd hardwired everything and instructed the 'bots to ignore broadcast signals.

At the time I assumed that he must have sabotaged our hard wires and our "ignore broadcasts," so he could access our system. With what I know now, I doubt it. I think he just used those megawatts to induce currents in our hardwires, currents that overrode our own commands.

Well his equipment was obviously pirate equipment and all our misgivings about his past were no longer uncertain. We were, however, mystified about why he bothered to call in his buddies when he could easily have done the dirty work himself and used our own boat to push his prize wherever he wanted it. Dad was still swearing softly and pounding his fist on his console. Mom had tears welling up and breaking off the ends of her lashes when she blinked. Gen was pale as a ghost and probably would've been screaming if she could have got her breath.

For some reason I wasn't scared this time. I think at that point I was only feeling betrayed and depressed. The same guy I'd been admiring and looking up to, he'd just been confirmed as a malevolent criminal. Sure, I'd been worried about him when we'd discovered the artifact, but at that time there'd only been the *possibility* that even a nice guy like him might kill us all in order to take the alien spaceship for himself.

The pirate shut down thrusters, made a few small correction pushes and tight beamed us. "Cooperate and live. Fight and die! What's it gonna be?"

Their boat was a skeletal frame of foam steel beams in the shape of a cube. At each of the eight corners were big, gimbal mounted thrusters so that four or five of them could push simultaneously in any chosen direction. This allowed sudden course deflections, useful for fighting, but not for much else. There were life modules scattered throughout the frame as well as laser modules around the periphery and load points for the attachment of prizes and booty. I know now that each module was set up to be completely self-contained and able to work independently. In theory, you could shoot out all but one thruster, one life module, and one laser and that ship could *still* kill you and take your valuables, though it'd be slow moving with only one thruster.

The ugly thing started to drift toward the Rock with all of the big lasers that could train on us—even some from the other side, aiming through gaps in the open frame—pointed our way. It was hard to see the details of its structure because it had a good light and radar absorptive coat on it to make it hard to track. I had no doubt there was a good laser reflective coat right under the absorptive one.

I was wondering how long it would take them to burn the artifact out of Mom's hiding place. I figured only an hour or so with Sander to show them where to cut. There really wasn't much we could do. We wouldn't even be able to try to track them since Sander would surely destroy all our tracking equipment. They'd probably take our boat. It'd keep us from chasing them and provide a little more prize money, a win-win for them.

Then we'd need a rescue, something we'd have to pay through the nose for. In a period of just a few days we'd gone from moderately well-off, to unbelievably wealthy, and now down to dirt poor.

Sander's voice came on the radio. "That you Jonesy? Looks like your piece of crap boat. This is Sandman."

There was a period of silence, then a suspicious tone "Sandman?! How did you get here?!" There was a little pause, then, "And *where* the hell have you been?"

"I turned respectable. I'm a miner. *This* is where I work now."

The guy on the other end chortled, "Sure Sandman. Well I'll tell you what. I'll let you in for a standard cut even if you *did* piss out on us."

Sander's voice sounded like large bubble foam-steel grating against a 'roid. "Maybe you didn't hear me. I turned respectable. My cut of the artifact is 25%, which is, I must point out, a hell of a lot bigger than your 'standard' cut." Sarcasm was dripping by the end of the sentence.

"Standard cut's a lot bigger than 25% of nothing."

"I've got my 'caster."

"Shit!"

Sander said, "You boys need to shove off 'fore you get hurt."

I was stunned, there'd been a tremor in the pirate's voice.

Sander's voice took on a kind of hopeful tone. "Go on home. No hard feelings."

The pirate's lasers opened up… At least some of them did. My screen went blank indicating that the laser I was supposedly controlling had just been burned out.

One second later the battle was over. Not only did all of our lasers discharge, but about two thirds of the pirates' lasers pivoted and fired on the ones that Sander didn't already have in his control. The thrusters on the pirate gimbaled over and opened up. A few minutes later the pirate was spinning at hundreds of RPM. A few modules tore loose and flew off into space and the ship itself began to drift away. My brain was spinning at the same speed as the pirate ship. The Sandman?!?!

To me the Sandman was the ultimate tale of genius gone bad. The only 'roid pirate whose name was a household word. He supposedly could control ten 'puters simultaneously by age five. He'd practically invented power-casters himself and, after inventing the skull ring interfacer, became an irresistible menace. Tales of piracy, plunder, fast living and loose morals were abundant.

Maybe you're thinking that a name like "Sander" should have been a tipoff, but I would never even have considered the Sandman and the quiet little man who'd been living with us in the same frame of reference.

Sander's voice came back on the radio with a tone of sad weariness. "Sorry folks. I don't really need any money from your artifact. I'll hang close for a while to help you out in case any more pirates come to visit, then I'll be moving on."

A minute later his voice came back on, this time by tight beam laser. I realized that he'd used radio for all of his previous communications so that everyone, including other pirates and belters, would know what was going on. He spoke in a near monotone this time. To my parents, he said, "Bob, Evelyn, I've truly enjoyed the hospitality you provided and my time with your family. You've confirmed for me that there really *are* decent people out there in this ol' universe. As I said, I don't need my share of whatever comes from the artifact. But, I'd appreciate your using my 25% in a good cause or donating it to some charity.

He spoke to my little sister next, "Gen, I hope you'll always stay as sweet and friendly as you've been to me."

There was a pause, long enough that I felt disappointed that he didn't have any words for me. This was even though I thought that perhaps being ignored by the Sandman might be a good thing. Then he said hoarsely, "Jimbo…" and the memory of him singling me out of the family through the emotion in his voice still chills me. He paused again. When he continued, he said "The money from that artifact is gonna make you rich and let you do things very few other people can do. You're young and you're gonna use the power that money brings you unwisely sometimes." He sighed, "*No one* can stop that from happening. But, I want you to try to take some advice from your old friend Sander. When I was *far* too young to use it wisely, I also got a lot of power and money. I *destroyed* a million things that meant the

23

world to me by abusing the power that was given to me…" his voice cracked again. "I used the power I had for all kinds of terrible things kid. Things I'm… so ashamed of. Things that drove away the people I loved. Things that ruined the lives of countless good people."

There was a long pause. During that time my mind went around in circles about whether I should reply to Sander, the man I'd looked up to for so long, or freeze out the Sandman, a man I thought was vile. I looked at my parents, thinking they'd give me some indication what to do, but their wide eyes made it look like they didn't have a clue.

Sander's voice came back on, "Money and power kid, they're not all they're cracked up to be. They won't make you handsome; they won't make you tall; they won't buy you love; they won't win you respect… If you want to be loved and respected; and believe me, we *all* do…" His voice became even throatier, "You've got to *be* lovable, and *act* respectably. I've learned to love you Jimbo, like the son I could never have. I've learned to admire you and your family for your human decency. I've hoped that you've loved and respected ol' Sander… even though no sane human being could respect… the man I *used* to be. But, if you ever did have any esteem for ol' Sander, I hope you'll take this bit of advice—*don't* go down the path I traveled."

At this point, with tears in my eyes I finally tried to reply. I don't remember what I said. I don't know if he shut off his receiver or just didn't want to talk any more, but he didn't answer me. We beamed and radioed him constantly for a while, but he never answered. He simply loaded a few of his things in his little boat and vectored off a ways. Then, as promised, he waited while we loaded up the alien artifact and followed us a while until he must've figured we were safely on our way back to Earth.

\*\*\*

Sander stopped in to see me once when I was twenty five. He just showed up at the house with a few bulbs of his microgravity beer. I was pretty rich by then and had a massive security system on the house to keep out the unwanteds.

Of course it didn't stop *him*.

I came home and found Sander sitting on my couch. At first I was startled and a little frightened, but then I recognized him. Tears in my eyes, I clapped my arms around him and just held onto him for a while.

We got a little tipsy on his beer, then went out on the town, me wearing a little disguise to keep people from recognizing me. We sat on the beach for an hour or two, then dropped by the local slum and looked at the school that I'd set up for the kids there. I'd named it "Sander's School" and no one ever figured out why. Sander and I talked for a while with little Joe Brooks, a kid I'd kind of taken under my own wing.

I called up Mom, Dad, and Gen and we all went out to dinner. You should've seen their eyes when they got to the table and recognized Sander. It was simple Italian food, but it was the finest meal and the best time of my life.

The proudest moment I've ever had was at the door just before Sander left.

"Jimbo," he called me once again, "you turned out well. You've always had my love," his eyes glistened, "now you have my respect." He turned and walked away into the night.

It's been twenty years now and I often wonder if he's still alive. I know he committed some terrible crimes when he was young and no one will, or should, forgive him those.

But, I just want people to understand.

He did some good too.

I suspect he did a lot more good than we'll ever know.

**The End**

Inspired (distantly) by the movie Shane.

# EXCELTOR

PROLOGUE

Life, in one form or another, has been around since before the Milky Way galaxy formed. Just as bacteria can be found on almost any unsterilized surface on Earth, once life first started, it populated everything it could grow on. When planetary bodies that life had populated are blown up and spread around by supernovas, the life that grew on them is also spread throughout the reaches of space in the form of sporulated single-celled organisms. These spores drift out of space—alone or on fragments of rock—to begin replicating wherever favorable conditions are found.

Two common types of self-replicating molecules, DNA and LSA, populate the uncommon, small, liquid-water temperature planets of the Milky Way. Though occasionally both life-forms *begin* to populate a suitable world, the metabolism of LSA life-forms either require or excrete some quantities of cyanide, while DNA life either requires or excretes oxygen, a molecule which is equally toxic to LSA forms.

Thus the two life forms are mutually incompatible. Eventually only one form of life succeeds on a particular planet.

Although the life-forms that evolve on DNA and LSA planets are quite different from one another, both of these molecules tend to repeatedly evolve remarkably similar life-forms on their own planets, similar to the way that Australia evolved many parallel species even though it was separated from Earth's other continents. Additionally, in more recent epochs, intelligent life-forms of both types have repeatedly developed Vinzearian physics, which, using high temperature superconductors, allows the opening of "wormholes" that can connect interstellar distances.

Intelligent life, using such interstellar wormholes, have repeatedly moved species from one planet to another. Occasionally these movements lead to mass extinctions secondary to the introduction of a particularly virulent microbe. Such events are often associated with a "sudden discontinuity" in the evolutionary record as the newly arrived species take over and diversify.

Recently (several millions of years), in this arm of our spiral galaxy, there have been several waves of intelligent "humaniforms" on the DNA worlds and "kranes" on the LSA worlds. Using Vinzearian physics, these intelligent beings spread to the worlds that would sustain them. As they did so, they also spread the more advanced, though unintelligent, life-forms from their home planets. Thus, widely spaced planets are frequently populated with closely-related species.

As incompatible as the self-replicating molecules that they are based on, the intelligent species have repeatedly warred and frequently reduced each other to pre-civilized states. They constantly attempt to procure more worlds for their own form of life.

Now, tens of thousands of years after a particularly virulent war, humaniforms and kranes have recently burst back on the interstellar scene. Encounters between them resulted in some initial wars, but then the two different types of intelligent beings established an uneasy truce regarding planets which had already been populated with *intelligent* life of one form or the other.

The race is on however, to find planets *without* intelligent life and "convert" such worlds from LSA to DNA or from DNA to LSA.

Sometimes, there are disagreements about whether advanced life forms of the other type *are* actually intelligent...

THE STORY

DEEP SPACE — 0.096 LIGHT YEARS FROM SOL

A featureless, 200 meter long cylinder, 7.1 meters in diameter hung motionless in space. A 7.15 meter diameter ring at one end was its only ornament. The ring suddenly coruscated to arc welder brilliance and shot down the length of the cylinder.
If a man could have seen past the incredibly brilliant light and through the ring, he would perhaps have recognized by the increased brightness of Sol that the other side of the ring was closer to Terra's star. In fact, space on the other side of the ring's wormhole was only 40 light minutes from our sun.
The cylinder was gone. Just the ring was left, tumbling lazily end over end, glowing a dull red from the energy that had poured through it. Cables trailed back away from the center of the ring, their ends sheared off to a mirror-polished surface where they'd been cut as the wormhole closed on them.

40 LIGHT MINUTES FROM SOL

Twenty degrees behind Jupiter, but nearly in Jupiter's same orbit, a 7.15 meter wormhole flashed into being and a 200 meter cylinder shot out at a velocity that laid it into a relatively stable solar orbit. The "ship" was a dead black structure, foamed out of a nickel steel asteroid in weightless deep space, cut to a perfect cylinder, tunneled into compartments, coated with energy absorptive layers, filled with sophisticated equipment and then named "Exceltor." Despite its highly light absorptive surface, the incredibly brilliant light from the wormhole ring reflected outward to cast it in sharp detail for a brief instant.

The other ends of the transected cables from the wormhole ring floated behind the ship for a moment and then began to reel in. A second later the surface of the ship began to sprout an extraordinary number and variety of antennas and parabolic reflectors. These began to rotate in various search patterns, gathering data from across the electromagnetic spectrum.

BRIDGE—HUMANIFORM CRUISER EXCELTOR—
5.2 AU (JUPITER'S DISTANCE) FROM SOL
0640 Eastern Standard Time (EST)

The brilliant flash of the wormhole ring was visible on some of the bridge sensors and signaled the shift. Captain Mario Leis whispered. "'Puter, all hands." Then in a resonant voice, he continued, "All right people, look sharp now, this is a new system. If there're any surprises I want us ready. Azimus, passive system survey, tell us what's out there. Smide get a shift-ring reloaded. We want everything running *quietly*. Anybody looks our way on *any part* of the EM spectrum; I want us to look as black as the inner aspects of your souls."

Leis listened to his station officers murmuring commands with some feeling of awe. He still found it hard to believe that the Exceltor and all these bright young people were his to command. He constantly had the feeling that he was too young for a rank that had only been given him because he'd made a couple of lucky decisions under fire. Still musing, he adjusted his head-ring and watched the image that Azimus was building in the holotanks in front of him.

The star in the center of the tank was labeled A2, indicating that it only deviated in small ways from those characteristics considered most desirable for human solar systems. Surprisingly, Azimus had already identified three reasonably-sized worlds—P1, P2, and P3—in or near the temperate zone. He'd also identified three gas giants farther out and a belt of asteroids between the two groups of planets. Probably a very rich system. Azimus was weaving and bobbing in his seat like he always did when concentrating. A little weird, Azimus was the best survey analyst Leis had ever worked with. Somehow Azimus used a 'puter in some strange fashion that extracted its very best. When given command of Exceltor and asked what he needed to be able to get the best out of the ship, Leis had insisted that Azimus be part of his crew.

"Sir! Heavy radio output from P2!" Azimus piped, voice crackling with excitement.

"Communicator Snellen, get on it," Leis barked. He saw to his embarrassment that Snellen was already murmuring rapidly to her 'puter and that P2 had already been flashing on her display of this solar system.

Leis looked back to his own display. P2 was now displaying a large moon. P2 was currently at about 130 degrees to the sun while his ship, the Exceltor, lay at 15 degrees. He noted that Exceltor's vector arrow was similar to the other bodies in the system.

"Navigation. Nice job of laying us in quietly." The kind of work Leis reliably obtained from Lieutenant Swayze. Leis wished *all* the personnel in Nav were as good. "Start placing transfer locators around P2. One into low orbit, one into a distant orbit and one for a medium distance, high speed bypass. Also place an escape transfer to P6 farside, eclipsed for P2."

"Engineering, how long 'til we can shift again?"

"Two more minutes, sir."

"When the new shift-ring is loaded how much of a jump will we have in the accumulators?"

"Only enough for sixty light minutes, sir."

"'Puter, display the solar temperate zone and the probable orbit for P2," he murmured. The display filled in a green donut for the temperate zone. It lay just outside the orbit line drawn for P2. As he looked at it the green donut faded and was replaced by a smaller diameter donut, in which P2's orbit lay pretty well centered. The 'puter spoke in his ear "P2 has a very large moon which has pulled off more atmosphere than most planets that size. The temperate zone has now been adjusted for a thinned atmosphere, secondary to the large moon, with a diminished greenhouse effect." Leis contemplated this new information. P2 would likely have temperatures in the liquid water range, but the thin atmosphere would be hard to breathe. The 'puter had now boxed off a corner of the display for data on P2. This showed a small sphere in light blue with an atmosphere ring in green, indicating free water and an oxygen atmosphere!

P2 was a DNA world!

Snellen turned her head to look back at Leis, "Captain, the radio output of P2 is multiple band, modulated. We are dealing with at least late pre-space technology. I would judge from some of the narrowly-beamed frequencies that have passed our position that they were beamed at satellites. The decoder is working on trying to convert to audio, 2-D or 3-D, but it may be a while yet before it works out what modulation systems they are using."

*Damn*, Leis thought, *such a promising system too.* If the decoder hadn't already deciphered the modulation system, it wasn't any known human variant. He whispered to the 'puter to give him all hands, "All hands, this is the captain. We're going to be sitting at silent stations for quite a while. This is an occupied system. Not one of ours, but we've found a DNA world with some fairly advanced technology. We've got some analysis time ahead to figure out just who's in the system. Until then we're going to be running quiet." He turned his head, "Mr. Swayze, you have command. Call me when we have data requiring further decisions."

As he headed for his bunk, Leis worried about whether the bridge crew would think him lazy for heading to his cabin. Or would they appreciate a break—out from under his eye—a chance to think on their own?

Common questions ran through his mind. Did the crew respect his achievements, or did they also think he'd simply been lucky? What about some of the crew who were nearly his own age. Should he have screened the crew to eliminate them and their possible jealousies, or did he desperately need their experience?

He was still mulling these questions when he fell asleep.

KRANE FLICKERSHIP—LYING IN SOL'S
ASTEROID BELT
0710 EST

"Lieutenant!" Both of the monitor's head-hands darted around, cilia writhing, eye clusters fully extended with excitement. "I've just picked up a Human shift-flash—size of flash about right for a cruiser—forty light minutes out from the sun, fifteen degrees, on the ecliptic, sir!"

"Communicator!" the lieutenant said sharply.

"Yes sir!"

"Message the flag with that data. Now! Red! Send it with an alarm!"

BRIDGE—KRANE FLAGSHIP—LIGHT CARRIER
XAJION—EARTH ORBIT
0711 EST

Commander Kinjie barely noticed the flashing light associated with another incoming message at the small "communications" wormhole array in the rear of his bridge. His head-hands darted around quickly though, when he heard the angry buzz of the alarm. The indicator was lighting one of the cables that connected through 3mm wormholes to the various flickerships he'd deployed about this system for observation posts and survey work. He looked back to his screen as the message played across it. *A humaniform cruiser! How could they have known we were in this system?! Coincidence?* The krane were well aware that the humans were also working hard to stake out systems in this unclaimed sector of space. The claws of all six of his feet were kneading the fabric of his "saddle-seat." Kinjie turned towards his operations officer. "Have any of our ships shifted or produced any significant EM radiation in the last hour?"

"No sir."

Kinjie turned again, "Communications! Red alarm messages, all ships, 'At least one human ship in system. Do *not* think it's aware of us. No shifting. Run quiet. Watch on all passive systems. Await further orders.'"

"Operations?"

"Yes sir?"

"Start locating transfers for two possible actions. One, all ships shift out system to safe rendezvous. Two, all ships shift to saturate area of human ship's probable location."

*Damn, damn, damn, damn… how could we have such bad luck?* Kinjie thought to himself. His left head-hand sank down to scratch the feeding orifice on the top of his carapace as he pondered the options for a while. They couldn't leave a rich system like this just because it was populated with a humaniform race and a single human ship had shown up. Eradication of the primitive humaniforms and other DNA based life-forms on the planet wouldn't be difficult and *one* humaniform cruiser certainly couldn't frighten a krane light carrier and her escorts. But—and this was a big but—if the human Federation *already* knew about the humaniforms here and this was a regular visit or part of a larger force he could be in deep diplomatic trouble.

Well, there was nothing to do except wait for the human to move and thus show its head-hand.

BRIDGE—HUMANIFORM CRUISER EXCELTOR—
5.2 AU FROM SOL
0850 EST

Feeling refreshed from his little nap, Leis said, "Well Mr. Swayze, what have you got for me?"

"Sir, Lieutenant Snellen has developed 2-D visual images and audio signals from P3. There don't seem to be any 3-D transmissions, though not all signal types have been successfully analyzed as yet. Sir, the visuals show humaniforms! The chest cavities are quite large as you might expect for a world with such a thin atmosphere. From the appearance of the images, the DNA-based life on this world has evolved familiar appearing species that fill similar ecological niches to those back in our home worlds. Many species were probably dropped off by earlier DNA star travelers. The medic says, however, that the humaniforms and some primates appear to be so similar to us that he would bet that P3 was colonized 50,000 to 100,000 years ago, just before the collapse."

"P3?"

"Yes sir. According to orbital analysis there's a small planet, P1, hidden behind the sun, so we've shifted all the P numbers up accordingly."

Swayze glanced back at the holo, "P3 is the only one from which we've detected any evidence of technology and that includes its large moon. P3 has an abundance of artificial satellites, many of which seem to be used for communications. Very few of the satellites, however, are large enough that they are likely to be occupied. It seems almost certain that they haven't rediscovered Vinzearian physics or shift technology. The satellites were probably launched with old-style rocket technology."

Swayze gestured at the blown up image of P3 in the back corner of the main holo. "P3 has a *lot* of water and several major landmasses. It seems to have a large number of different languages.

"A disproportionate amount of 2-D with accompanying audio comes from this landmass—he lit it up—that they call 'North America.' Because a large part of the 2-D from there is for entertainment, it's been relatively easy for the 'puters to analyze the language they speak there, called English. The computer's translation algorithm is already up to 5,000 words.

"P3 doesn't appear to have established a planet-wide government. Instead we believe there are at least 20 and perhaps several hundred separate governments. The government of the North American landmass appears to be a democracy and, judging from the amount of criticism leveled at it by the press, not very repressive." He glanced uncomfortably at Leis, "Um, we've picked up one 2-D image of what appeared to be a nuclear explosion."

Leis gave him a grim look, but only said, "Go ahead."

"The system is incredibly rich. Both P2 and P4 could probably be made livable. Except for its thin atmosphere, P3 is almost perfect. The belt of asteroids is likely heavy in metals and a *huge* bonus is P3's satellite." Ticking on his fingers, "It's already bordering the temperate zone, it's *close* to a livable planet and it's *very* large for a moon."

"Well, Mr. Swayze, what are your recommendations?" Swayze was expecting this question. The captain considered it an important part of officers' training to demand decision recommendations from his staff before issuing his own commands. Woe be upon the officer who made a recommendation which the captain considered to be reckless or ill considered. However, *not having* a recommendation was considered to be almost as bad. "Sir, as the krane are actively surveying this region, it's only a matter of time before they find this fertile system. As in the Saltan incident they are not likely to view the destruction of humaniforms not affiliated with the Federation as a violation of the current treaty and in fact would probably rapidly proceed with sterilization of P3 so that they could begin repopulating with LSA life-forms."

Mention of the Saltan homeworld produced leaden stomachs all over the bridge. Most of the crew had lived through Exceltor's inability to prevent the deaths of millions of sentients during the kranes' sterilization of that planet.

*At least we arrived here in plenty of time,* Leis thought.

Swayze continued, "I would recommend making a command decision that the Federation *will* wish to protect these people and that in order to do so it will need to enter into a treaty with them. The most rapid way to accomplish this goal would be for us to establish contact with one of the governments on P3, and then immediately return to Avajan with a small group of their diplomats. Fleet could then dispatch a group to provide protection to P3 during the negotiations."

"Agreed," Leis said.

Swayze glanced at his screens, "Sir, the accumulators have stored enough energy for a shift to P3 with a backup shift of 7 light months. I recommend that we use a shift I've had positioned behind that big moon. We'd shift in at a velocity which will bring us almost immediately out of the moon's shadow in a high speed flyby cometary orbit. During the flyby we should use passive sensors to more closely inspect and evaluate P3. At some point during that orbit we can open a small port to the surface in order to make contact and pick up a diplomat. That orbit will also give us time to complete charging the accumulators for a shift to Avajan. If we need to shift unseen so as not to frighten the general populace, we can just wait until we arrive back behind their moon before departing."

Leis gave him a warm smile, "Excellent, Mr. Swayze. Prepare your plan for execution, proceed when ready." He turned towards the communications team, "Lieutenant Snellen. Have you located the head of government of this North America?"

*Like finding the proverbial grain of sand,* she thought to herself. "Sir, there seem to be several countries in North America, but the most populous is known as the United States and the head of its government is usually located in one building. The 'puter is currently trying to pinpoint its location."

BRIDGE—KRANE FLAGSHIP—LIGHT CARRIER
XAJION—EARTH ORBIT
0855 EST

Kinjie spun his saddle-seat and raised his heads to examine the intruder on his bridge. *Diplomats!* He thought with fury. He couldn't understand why the empire had seen fit to load him with such unwanted baggage. Even worse to give this *degenerate* titular control of a simple military mission to sterilize a DNA planet. Just because there were a few DNA humaniforms on it, the empire sends a diplomat "in case of political problems." Now, even worse, merely

38

twelve hours into the actual mission, Federation humans had arrived to provide a situation that *could* be construed as a diplomatic problem.

Quell's cilia were writhing above his fully extended heads and a scritching sound came from under him where his footclaws kneaded the steel deckplates.

"*Why* wasn't I informed of the human ship's arrival?"

"I was waiting to collect more information"

"And now that you have?"

"The human ship arrived two hours and 15 minutes ago. We picked up the arrival one hour and 45 minutes ago because it arrived at a point 30 light minutes from the nearest flickership. No further human ships have arrived and it has not moved. Thus it's probably alone and currently carrying out analysis."

"And why didn't you attack it at once?"

"Because, I felt it wise to wait to determine whether it *was* accompanied and whether it would proceed directly to P3 suggesting previous knowledge of these humaniforms." Kinjie continued frostily, "I might point out that either of these two possibilities could have presented you with considerable diplomatic difficulty."

Quell regarded him but did not appear chastened.

"Yes, well, what if this human ship immediately shifts back to Federation space with its findings?"

Kinjie stared at the diplomat for a moment, then decided to bury him in analysis. "Analysis of its shift-flash has been carried out by a flickership which was situated farther from its arrival site and had time to align a telescope on the arrival site prior to arrival of the light wave-front. Its shift-ring diameter of about seven meters suggests a human cruiser. Spectral analysis indicates it's using General Superconductor Products' shift-rings. Those rings are usually associated with high quality construction at the shipyards at Lissholm or Taynome. Shift-ring reflection analysis of the cruiser body itself leads us to believe it is probably the Humaniform Federation cruiser Exceltor. Flash brilliance indicates it just made a 'zeroing in jump from about 0.1 light years out. Assuming a Federation warship's usual one percent jump error, the original jump was ten light years. We know the humans' accumulator charge rates are poor. Their storage rates only give them about 60,000 additional discharge megawatts every hour, *and* their capacities are relatively low. So, unless it sat out there at 0.1 lights and fully recharged its accumulators, it won't have enough charge on board for a ten light year return shift for at least 8 more hours."

Kinjie thought Quell had had a hard time following his explanation, but the diplomat didn't admit it. Instead, he said, "What's your plan then?"

Kinjie decided to *keep* telling the diplomat more than he probably wanted to know or could comprehend. "Unfortunately our surveillance records indicate that Exceltor is recently under the command of a Captain Leis. He has a well-founded reputation for causing us trouble completely out of proportion to his resources. This has however, resulted in excessively rapid promotion and he is relatively new to the command of cruisers. In addition, he *cannot* know we're here in this system since we hadn't had any shift activity for the hour before his arrival, and he arrived less than one light hour from our farthest position. I see this as a prime opportunity to rid ourselves of an annoying commander, a Federation cruiser, and an entire world full of humaniforms in one simple operation."

Quell's head-hands paused their motions and his footclaws stopped grating on the deck. Kinjie thought the sudden immobility was likely due to hidden excitement over the possibility of such a coup. Kinjie continued, "I expect that Leis' plan will be to move to P3 orbit and try to make diplomatic contact with the retrogressed humaniforms there. As we're already in orbit about P3 we should have the advantage of surprise and we will be able to destroy him without difficulty."

"But you have only the one ship in P3 orbit! The others are at P2 and 4! If he's *lucky* he might destroy us!"

"He has a cruiser! Xajion is a light carrier! We have the advantage of surprise!" Kinjie gave Quell a disparaging look, "We'll destroy him, don't worry. In any event, as soon as we see his incoming shift-flash, we'll message the two destroyers and they'll immediately shift here as well, then it'll be three on one."

Quell's cilia relaxed. Grudging respect for the well-known Commander Kinjie won over his anger. His heads dropped a little from their fully extended positions. "What if he does nothing but wait to shift back to Federation territory?"

"If he does nothing for the next six hours we'll shift to his location and destroy him there."

"Why not do that now?"

"Because," Kinjie said with a contemptuous wave of his left head-hand, "we're at *least* fifteen minutes behind on his activities. If he had a high velocity on transfer, or if he made a shift during the last fifteen minutes, we could arrive to find nothing *and* lose the advantage of surprise." He stared Quell down, "Warfare is *my* business. Surprise is the most powerful weapon we have in shift warfare. If you know where your enemy is going, and even better are waiting there for him, you have gripped him by his reproductive organs."

Quell said nothing for about twenty seconds, then, "Very well, I'll wait with you."

*Excretions!* Kinjie thought. "I'll tolerate your interference and follow your recommendations *until* battle is joined. Once a fight begins, *I'll* be in command and I'll brook no interference."

41

After a moment, Quell grudgingly said, "Agreed."

"Captain. We're ready to execute."
"Thank you Mr. Swayze."
Leis contemplated his words for a moment so as to
sound more assured and "in command," then
murmured, "'Puter, all hands... All hands, we're
shifting to a location behind P3's moon. The
humaniform population there will be eclipsed and
won't see our shift-flash. They don't appear to have
Vinzearian physics and so no form of shift technology.
Nonetheless they do have other forms of
sophisticated technology *including* nuclear weapons.
I'll advise you all to remember the Latus incident ... a
lack of shift technology does *not* make them ignorant
savages and the fact that they are DNA humaniforms
does *not* necessarily make them friendly. They could
be dangerous and I *don't* want them to know we're
here. We will run quiet *and* alert."
"Lieutenant Snellen, immediately upon arrival in P3
orbit, you and Gunner Nedcam will locate this White
House and their president, then set up to transfer a
party of three to that location."
Snellen nodded.
"Engineer Smide, are all antennas stowed and the
ship's exterior clean for shift?"
"Yes sir."
"Good, you will initiate a fast reload of another shift-
ring after we arrive. If needed, I want to be able to
shift away from P3 immediately..." he gave a grim
chuckle, "or sooner."
Leis turned, "Mr. Swayze, immediately upon arrival
you will locate escape transfers, one max jump and

one to P5 farside. You may now proceed with the shift to the backside of P3's moon."

As he heard the rumble of the shift-ring running down the length of his ship, Leis saw Snellen frowning at a bright red message on her holo. The bright flash from the shift lighted numerous instruments on the bridge as she turned. Her voice trembled, "Captain! The 'puter's analysis of 2-D news shows from North America has noted several reports of an extremely brilliant broadband light flash in P3's near space about seven hours ago! They don't know what it is—it isn't ours—some kranes may already be here!"

Resisting the temptation to swear at such news, Leis said in steady tones that surprised even himself, "'Puter, all hands... Battle stations! Battle stations! Presumed krane ship already in orbit about P3! Let's figure out where she is, no active systems, no EM radiation. All antennas deployed must be set for rapid collapse." He studied the holo for a moment, then spoke to his bridge personnel, "They may not know we're near P3 because our shift-flash should have been screened by the moon," he shrugged, "though they should have had observation ports back here. Place our own observation ports behind the moon, on the other side of P3, in between P3 and the moon and on the surface of Exceltor. Ship surface observers to notify me if they think they *might* have seen an approaching locator port, even if they're pretty sure it was really only a meteoroid strike on our surface."

Leis felt good that he'd managed to keep his voice relatively calm through that whole set of commands. He wondered at how his team managed to look calm as well and wondered if perhaps he'd fooled them into thinking he had it all under control. Maybe they couldn't tell how hard his heart was thumping. "'Puter, bridge... That krane bastard sure as *hell* knows we're in the system 'cause our original shift-flash got here two hours and 45 minutes ago. Azimus, you're going

to be able to see him in the reflected light from this
moon and we know that his passive gear isn't going to
work very well looking back toward the moon as we
come out from behind it." *Damn, damn, damn, damn!*
Leis thought, then managed to continue, still surprised
at how calm he sounded, "Let's hope he's not on the
opposite side of P3, 'cause we need to find him *now*.
"Snellen, as soon as you and Nedcam find that
president, snatch him. We'll talk to him here."
"'Puter, how many words in your translation
vocabulary now?"
"Thirteen thousand sir."

GUNNERY ROOM—HUMANIFORM CRUISER
EXCELTOR—COMETARY EARTH ORBIT
0905 EST

Nedcam flipped his holocube image away from the 2-
D pix of the president, thinking that this would be the
first time *his* shiftgun had been used to kidnap a head
of state. A glance at his panel showed all green. He
started his scope. His holocube showed the sparkling
lights of a P3 city beneath the opening of the port-
ring. The minuscule port-ring had the snout of a
hololens protruding a mere tenth of a millimeter. At
this height and small size, no one should have seen
the little flash when it opened. He sent it rocketing
toward the surface and then began to track laterally.
He recognized the Washington monument from some
of the 2-D pictures that Snellen had fed him. *Right
city!* He settled down to the tedious business of
looking for the White House. No maps on any of the
2-D entertainment programs picked up so far... Wait
was that it?
Yes!
Nedcam felt incredibly lucky that the White House
was so close to the monument. He sent his hololens
approaching at high speed.

44

WHITE HOUSE—WASHINGTON DC
0911 EST

A minuscule, faintly-glowing port-ring slid up to the door of the White House. Turning the orientation of the port-ring so that he was looking up, Nedcam slid the tenth millimeter sliver of protruding hololens under the door and into the hallway. It rose to the ceiling and moved down the hall, looking for areas that looked active and hoping he could recognize the voice of the president from the audio recordings Snellen had sent him. Because the atmosphere on this planet was much thinner, the recordings of the president's voice sounded very deep.

There! Nedcam and Snellen actually *saw* the president, walking down the hall towards the hololens. He was accompanied by a couple of men in uniforms and a man in clothing Snellen said they called a "suit." Nedcam held the lens stationary as they came toward it. He knew that the 1 mm diameter wormhole was only emitting a hundredth of a watt and so the hololens would be difficult to see, but he suspected that, like most other humaniforms, their retinas were very sensitive to motion. After the men went by, the lens fell in just above and behind their heads and followed as they turned off into a large room marked "Secure".

Even before they were seated at the long table the president was asking questions. "What the *hell* do you mean 'we don't know what it is'? I thought that was what we spent all the money on space radar for? Just last month you told me you knew the location and function of every significant bit of space junk out there, and *now* you tell me that a flash *so bright* that it was seen *all over this hemisphere* came from some object directly above the North American continent that you *didn't even know* was there?"

"Well, ahh, Mr. President it is a *very* black object with a very strange radar silhouette."

"And what's that supposed to mean?"

"Well, being black it's extremely difficult to see with optical sensors. The radar silhouette is very faint, but appears extremely large. It appears to be at least six times larger than the space station, which is the biggest thing ever launched into orbit. I suspect that any operator who's seen it in the past has simply assumed it to be a glitch in the system."

"Six times larger?!"

"Well, yes sir. Actually it appears very long and narrow. But we suspect that someone has simply discovered a way to electronically alter an object's radar return from small and dense to large and dim. A neat trick, I'm afraid and one we'll have to be on the lookout for in the future."

"Hell, Damn and Spit! And what was the bright flash? Some kind of nuclear weapon?"

"Oh, No sir. There was no radiation or EMF, sir. We don't know what it was."

Nedcam was working furiously to set up his transfer-ring. The four men were too close together for him to pick the president off alone, no matter how he angled a ring and no matter where he started and stopped its travel. The flash from a ring big enough to get them all would crisp the remaining occupants of the room.

*Ah,* two of the group of four stepped away to a 2-D viewscreen on a side table and then the president stepped very close and began talking quietly into the ear of the uniformed man. Nedcam could take them both with the 1.5 meter transfer-ring. There! He had it lined up and ready to track. Waiting, waiting, everyone in the room was starting to look away toward the big display screen at the end of the table. Now!

There was a loud bang and a blast of air that blew every paper off the table. Even though they were all

46

looking away, the men in the room were temporarily blinded by a brilliant flash of light. When they turned back, the carpeted floor had a 1.5 meter "crop circle" of closely trimmed fibers where President Rayland and General Price had been standing. A small oval of brown leather from the sole of the president's right shoe curled up and rocked back and forth just off center. For a moment everyone blinked and stared. Then alarms began to ring.

GUNNERY/TRANSFER ROOM—HUMANIFORM CRUISER EXCELTOR—COMETARY EARTH ORBIT 0915 EST

The president dropped a sudden inch, then stumbled to the side in the lower gravity. A blast of higher pressure air from the ship eddied little curls of carpet fiber around his feet. He and the General found themselves on a small pedestal in the center of a 1.5 meter ring that lay on the floor between two vertical rails. He could feel heat still emanating from the ring that appeared to have been the source of the blinding flash. He looked about, seeing that he was in a room with several similar rings of different diameters, all of them also on rails.

The computer translated for Lt. Snellen and synthesized her voice speaking English. "President Rayland, I'm Lt. Snellen of the DNA humaniform spaceship Exceltor. I apologize for this rude abduction, but it's necessary that we move quickly. Please put on the mask you see on the table in front of you. The air pressure on board this ship is quite high compared to your planet's, so we need to supply you an altered mix containing helium in order to keep you safe."

The president felt a wavering sense of unreality about the whole thing. His entire worldview reeled. For a few seconds he'd feared that he might be going to pass out, but apparently the sensation of lightness he felt was because his weight had truly diminished. The hard evidence of his senses was incontrovertible. He was awake. He'd just been moved to a completely different location and environment in a flash of light. For his part, General Price took a few steps toward the bulkhead door, then returned uncertainly to stand next to his commander in chief.

Snellen's voice came on again, "Sirs, please. We need you to put on the breathing masks so I can equalize the compartment's pressure to the ships' and take you to the captain.

Neither of them said anything. Then President Rayland reached out, picked up the mask and put it on his face. The general frowned, "What if they're poisoning you?"

Rayland snorted, "It'd be a lot easier to just shoot me, wouldn't it?"

General Price hesitated another moment, then put on his own mask. With a whooshing sound the pressure started going up.

The president and his advisor began vigorously cracking their jaws as they tried to adjust to the painfully higher air pressure in the ship.

Rayland said, "Damn! My ears hurt. I was never any good at diving to depths more than a few feet."

Not knowing that a port in the mask supplied their breathing mixture, Price had been wondering if the masks really did anything, but the high pitch of Rayland's voice told him they really were breathing helium.

BRIDGE—HUMANIFORM CRUISER EXCELTOR—
COMETARY EARTH ORBIT
0916 EST

Azimus stopped weaving in his seat for a second and then turned to the captain. "Sir, there's a krane light carrier in low P3 orbit!"

*Damn! Damn! Damn!* Leis thought, *nothing but bad news!* "How'd you find it so fast?"

"Sir, at first I thought it was actively radiating. Instead it seems the locals are bouncing all kind of microwave frequencies off of it. I suspect *they're* just trying to figure out what it is, but they're lighting it up like a Sinto beacon. Do you want me to pass the location on to gunnery or are we getting out of this orbit?"

"If they can, have gunnery run some locator lenses over and sit them right on the surface of that bastard. Don't heat them yet, the treaty's in effect 'til they act in a hostile fashion or we reach an agreement with the humaniforms." Leis turned, "Swayze is that president on board yet?"

GUNNERY/TRANSFER ROOM—HUMANIFORM CRUISER EXCELTOR—COMETARY EARTH ORBIT 0920 EST

Lt. Snellen stepped in as soon as the air pressure in the transfer room stabilized at ship normal.
"Gentlemen, I'd like to take you forward to meet the captain."

The two men jerked back as they heard both Snellen's voice and the translation coming from overhead speakers. The General stepped between the president and the Lieutenant and they both goggled at the sight before them. The Lieutenant appeared human, yet, oddly alien. She was short, about 1.6 meters and had a wide pelvis, but a narrow chest. Her eyes were set a little too far apart, her hair was *very* light blond, almost white and was combed back from an extremely low hairline that almost merged with her brows. She looked mammalian or at least had masses of flesh in the same locations as human mammaries, though they looked odd on her small chest. She had no apparent weapon visible. General Price said, "*What* the hell are *you* and how do you know our language?"

"I apologize. I'm Lieutenant Snellen and I don't actually know your language, but our language computers have worked up a reasonable translation algorithm based on many hours of your 2-D video transmissions. Translations are being delivered from those computing resources." She held out some small objects, "If you'd put in these earbuds, the translation won't have to be broadcast from the overhead speakers. I'd like to explain all this in more depth, but time is very short."

President Rayland recovered his grip on whatever reality this was and in his usual assertive, confident style brushed the General aside to pick up an earbud. "Hell, General, if *these* people wanted to hurt me, they would've done it by now."

Thinking that her skin was too pale, the president followed Lieutenant Snellen out into an astonishingly long, narrow corridor. Her limbs seemed surprisingly thin, though still muscular. Despite all the oddities, he still felt sure somehow that this "Lieutenant" was a human female. Or some kind of human female anyway.

For her part, Snellen thought the earthmen's larger chest cavities and thick heavy legs made them look like aging bodybuilders who'd forgotten to work on their arms. She wasn't sure whether to appreciate or be concerned about the president's rapid assimilation of the situation and almost sudden cooperation.

BRIDGE—HUMANIFORM CRUISER EXCELTOR—
COMETARY EARTH ORBIT
0925 EST

As they walked quickly along the interminable corridor, the president and General Price passed several compartments filled with an incredible variety of odd human types on the way to the bridge. The bridge was the same. Numerous beings, all of whom appeared to be humanlike, but who varied widely from Earth normal, stared into three-dimensional images in the bridge.

Due to the fact that Earth had a thinner atmospheric density than any other known populated planet, all of them seemed to have small chests and pale skins. Thicker atmospheres on their home planets allowed smaller lungs and filtered out the UV which selected for additional melanin on Earth. Though they had small chests and pale skins in common, otherwise there was tremendous variety in size, shape and feature. As he looked around, President Rayland thought he saw some with similar variations, as if they might have come from the same sub-species.

A bald young man with a ring of short dark hair just above surprisingly small ears turned to face the president. "President Rayland, I am Captain Leis, commander of the Humaniform Federation's light cruiser Exceltor. We are very sorry to have abducted you, but your world appears to be in grave danger from an alien race known as the Krane."

Rayland gave the young captain a dubious look, "And I'm supposed to believe this, just on your say-so?"

Leis said, "No, though I fear we may not be able to prove it to your satisfaction. However, we do expect that you're aware of the arrival of a krane light carrier in Earth orbit a little more than seven of your hours ago. It would have arrived in a flash of energy easily visible at your planet's surface. Currently your planet is bombarding it with microwave radar and other imaging radiations. We expect that your people are trying to figure out what it is. To radar imaging techniques its appearance will be quite dim due to sophisticated absorption and diffusion techniques."

Rayland and the General glanced at one another as they thought about the commotion they'd just left at the White House. Then Rayland looked back at the captain and frowned, "We're *aware* of such an object. What kind of danger are you claiming it poses?"

Leis took a few moments to explain the presence of LSA and DNA life-forms in the galaxy as well as the ongoing battle between humaniforms and kranes for the small liquid water planets. "Both species are currently surveying star systems for suitable worlds and trying to protect worlds populated with their own life-forms." Leis shrugged, "Unfortunately, both are also trying to convert worlds populated with non-sentient species to make them suitable for their own life-forms."

General Price narrowed his eyes, "Convert?"

Leis nodded, "By wiping out all existing life and seeding the world with their own form of life."

The president's stomach lurched at the implication, but he didn't show it on his face. "But they wouldn't wipe out life on our planet because of the intelligent life there, correct?"

Leis got a pinched expression, "There's the problem. Defining what's intelligent or sentient is always open to interpretation. Kranes have been known to wipe planets populated with intelligent humaniforms, claiming that they believed the occupants to be no smarter than monkeys. Recently the Krane Empire agreed to a treaty with our Humaniform Federation protecting worlds belonging to either group. Unfortunately, that treaty does not extend to your planet because you are neither a member, nor a protectorate of our Federation. We think it likely that the krane carrier intends to sterilize your planet and begin seeding it with LSA forms *prior* to any chance that it might become a part of our Federation."

The president listened to both the captain speaking unintelligibly and the small voice translating in his ear with a sense of unreality. He did his best to show an outward calm despite a heart hammering in a chest become too tight. "I suppose that you feel that this krane carrier is capable of such a thing?" He wondered briefly to himself just why he even *began* to believe the captain's incredible story, but then reflected that, in view of what had just happened to his own person, he must either believe in the incredible—or find himself insane.

"There is no doubt," Leis responded solemnly.

"We've been assuming that some kind of electronic trickery has been making its radar image both dimmer and larger. How big *is* the damn thing in actuality?"

"Seven hundred thirteen meters long."

"Holy shit!"

The general turned and whispered to the president. "Sir that's not too big to nuke."

Making it obvious that he had heard and fully understood the general's whisper, the captain said "It *is* true that one of your nuclear weapons would readily destroy the krane ship, but the krane will have little difficulty destroying any rocket driven delivery systems. Do you have anything faster?"

An uncomfortable silence reigned while the president considered. He felt as if he was in a situation careening out of control. "Can you help us, and if so, how do we know that you actually *are* the guys in shining white armor?"

The small synthetic voice in the president's ear queried as to whether "guys in shining white armor" meant "helpful or good beings."

The president nodded.

Leis said, "Mr. President, we can enter into an agreement between you, as the highest available Earth authority, and myself, as the highest ranking member of the Humaniform Federation. Earth would become a protectorate, subject to later ratification by both sides. For such a protectorate treaty to be held valid requires at least token payment. One nickel iron asteroid of your choice, but greater than fifty-three meters on its smallest axis would be satisfactory. As evidence that we are indeed the good guys, this would come due only upon incontrovertible evidence that the krane intended to damage your planet and our successful intervention to prevent such an outcome."

"And what else would we owe afterward?"

"Nothing more would be owed. Once this immediate crisis has been resolved, you would then negotiate Earth's entry into the Humaniform Federation with a diplomatic team."

The president shrugged, "I'm happy to agree to have you protect our planet. A single asteroid which we can't currently use is well worth it. However, I won't agree to anything further until we know more. Can you print up a document for me to sign?"

"Sign? Oh! The computers have recorded your verbal agreement. That's sufficient." He got a grim look on his face, "Unfortunately, we may not be able to uphold our part of the bargain. Exceltor is only a cruiser. We are facing a krane light carrier which not only holds a host of smaller flickerships, but undoubtedly is escorted by one to three destroyers or possibly even some cruisers."

The president's eyes cast about the room for a moment. "Why don't you send for help?"

"I sorely wish that I could. The nearest help is nearly 12 light years away. Our shift inaccuracy of one percent means that a message capsule sent that far would have an average error in its arrival of 43 light days. Thus after arrival, its radio beacon would take weeks to arrive. We could go ourselves, but with shifts, recharging of our accumulators and correcting shifts it would be at least 36 hours before we might be able to return. The krane already know we're here and they will certainly see us depart. By the time we could return they would probably have destroyed most of your planet's ability to sustain DNA life-forms."

"Okay," President Rayland said, pale with dismay. His voice rasped, "Do the best you can for us."

Captain Leis gave a jerky nod then turned to the young woman beside him, "Ensign Mallor, escort our guests to the bridge visitor's seats and answer their questions."

The president retrieved the hand he had extended for a shake, but which the captain had not noticed. He and the general moved to the rear of the bridge with Mallor.

The crew on the long, narrow bridge all seemed busy at one task or another. The president couldn't avoid a subliminal feeling that they were all underdeveloped weaklings because of their small chests, but they appeared to be quite efficiently performing their assigned tasks. All had slender metallic halos about their heads, but rather than passing about their brows as with a biblical halo they passed obliquely over both the ears and mouth and presumably were the means by which their constant low volume murmurings were picked up by the computers. The personnel were arranged in ranked seats before the captain, facing away into tanks containing various three dimensional images. The arrangement was such that the captain could see over each of his officers' shoulders and into the officer's holocube. An enormous 3-D image hanging out in front of all of them appeared to represent the solar system.

Captain Leis had a hawk-like gaze which flashed here and there, pinning anything or anyone like insects inspected under a magnifying glass. "Lt. Snellen!" he barked, "Extrude an antenna near that moon and prepare to send a message to the krane as follows,

'Any krane vessels within this solar system, be aware that this humaniform planet is now a protectorate of the Federation of Humaniform Systems. Any move against this planet *or* its intelligent, sentient, humaniform inhabitants will be construed as a move against the Federation. Please remain stationary and communicate with us regarding your intentions in this system. Shifting your ships *will* be construed as a move of aggression if carried out prior to an agreement approving your method of departing this system."'

Close beside the moon a tiny flash of light signaled the opening of a small port-ring through which Snellen extruded an omnidirectional antenna to send the message, both in Human/common galactic and in Krane/spiral. The krane could translate readily, but a double translation left fewer opportunities for error.

"Gunny! This is the captain. We're about to stir up the krane... Do you have your locator lenses in place on the surface of their ship?

"Yes sir! We have two shift-ring cutters in place and penetrator rings set up over most of their accumulator banks."

"Be ready to fire those rings, on my command, or automatically if they light their shift-ring."

"Yes sir!"

"Azimus. Do you have observation ports behind every meteoroid in our vicinity?" A choked giggle rose from several of the bridge crew.

"All but one sir!"

"Snellen. Send the message."

WHITE HOUSE SITUATION ROOM
0930 EST

"And then he was just gone?!"

"Yes dammit! How many times do I have to tell you people the same story?"

56

In the other corner they'd just finished briefing the vice president. He looked at them dubiously, "So will this… thing, whatever it is, be able to get me too, even down here in the bunker?"

"Your guess is as good as ours Mr. Vice President. Do you think we should swear you in as President?" The VP scratched his balding pate. "You don't think he's still alive?"

"Damned if I know."

"Let's wait a while… *I* don't relish explaining *this one* to the press."

BRIDGE—KRANE FLAGSHIP—LIGHT CARRIER
XAJION—EARTH ORBIT
0930 EST

Commander Kinjie again heard the buzz of an alarm message. It was from the same scout ship in the asteroid belt. The humans had moved! Because of the delay for the light signal to reach the flickership's location in the belt they must have moved 30 minutes ago.

Where the Hell had the Motherless oitons gone? Somewhere within thirty to sixty light minutes by the size of the flash, yet someplace at least 15 light minutes from any of the krane ships or they would have seen the arrival flash already. Why would they go anyplace 15 light minutes away? Were they going to leave the system? If so, why? Any *idiot* could see it was a rich system! They couldn't know that the krane were already there… Could they?

"Sir! Radio message from behind that moon!"

"Behind the moon? Did that humaniform cruiser jump in back there?"

"Sir, I'll check sir." Duot's head-hands and their cilia were beginning to droop as he hunched over his instruments.

"You'll check! Why the Mother don't you know from the observation ports we have back there?"

"Um, Sir, We didn't have an observation port behind the moon sir."

"Didn't have an observation port!" Kinjie screeched, "What in the name of the Mother have you been *doing*?!" A sensation like trickling ice water began to run up inside the Commander's lower shell. "Did you think this was some kind of a *pleasure* cruise? Have you left out any other standard measures?"

Then the contents of the message popped up on the screens and both Kinjie's and Quell's cilia began writhing in fury.

Quell hissed, "They've snuck into your hindmost excretory orifice!"

"This is *now* a battle… get off my bridge!" Kinjie spun in his saddle, his head-hands extended to full height, "Duot, where the oiton is that cruiser? *Is* it behind that moon?"

"Just an antenna on line of sight sir!"

"I *said,* 'Where the hell *is* it?'"

"Sir, I don't know."

"Don't cower! Find it!"

"Sir! Working, Sir!" Duot and several other junior officers' head-hands swiveled back to their holocubes. Cold ice settled in Kinjie's gut. The Mother-be-damned humans *must* have jumped behind the moon. Why? They couldn't possibly have known he was here could they? What kind of orbit were they in? Shouldn't they already be out from behind the moon? Could they have *already* located his ship? No! Xajion was too stealthy, they couldn't have found her in just 15 minutes, but they might find her soon and he had *no damned idea* where *they* were.

"Gueel! Locate a jump to the side of this damn planet opposite that moon, low orbit."

"Nonise! Pull the Flickerships."

"Fotayl! Message capsules to Zoaden and Yaitan, send our records and tell them we're jumping out of the presumed line of sight of this damned humaniform cruiser."

A thrumming sound like a god beating a huge barrel signaled the back-shifting of the flickerships into their berths.

Duot timidly turned his saddle and said weakly, "Commander, the local humans have been bathing us with microwave radiation. We may be pretty easy to find."

Kinjie didn't hear. "Gueel! As soon as you've located, jump us the hell out of here!"

BRIDGE—HUMANIFORM CRUISER EXCELTOR—
COMETARY EARTH ORBIT
0935 EST

"Captain, they're jumping!"

"Fire, Dammit!"

"Captain, we fired, on auto as ordered!"

"Did you get 'em?"

"Looking sir."

"Pray to your gods that you did!"

BRIDGE—KRANE FLAGSHIP—LIGHT CARRIER
XAJION—EARTH ORBIT
0935 EST

Commander Kinjie heard the boom of opening, then the powerful thrumming of the shift-ring running the length of his ship.

But then the Mother struck Xajion a horrible blow. One that left her ringing like a massive bell. Blasting wind signaled decompression. Lights arced bright and went out.

Faint bangs signaled the closing of decompression doors in thinned atmosphere. A dim glow from the emergency lights brought back some visibility as the Xajion tumbled like a can kicked by a giant. Kinjie clung to his saddle with all six feet, cursing himself for a fool.

The humans had obviously cut his shift-ring during its passage along the ship. Thus, they'd cut his ship in half. The question was, how much was left in *his* half? He looked about in the dim glow noting with grim satisfaction that that damned diplomat Quell had been flung into a bulkhead and lay motionless. At least Kinjie wouldn't have to listen to that blithering idiot saying "I told you so," during his darkest hour.

BRIDGE—HUMANIFORM CRUISER EXCELTOR—
COMETARY EARTH ORBIT
0938 EST

"Captain! Part of the krane carrier is still in its original orbit. Spinning badly! We must have cut their shift-ring mid-transit!"

"Sir," Azimus called, "our observation ports on the other side of P3 picked up an incoming flash, presumably the jumped fragment."

"All hands…" Leis said, "OK crew, we've hurt that carrier. Don't know how badly. Good work, but there's bound to be support ships incoming. Look sharp! Stay passive. Don't, I repeat, DON'T, let *them* get the drop on us like we got the drop on them.'"

At the back of the bridge, the president and General Price blinked their eyes in the wake of the brilliant flash that had just lit so many of the holocubes in the bridge. "My God, Mallor, what's happening out there?"

The ensign blinked. "Well, I'm pretty sure we just cut the carrier's shift-ring mid transit, sir."

"We *heard* that part! What's it *mean*?"

The ensign stared at them, seemingly at a loss to explain. A small voice began to whisper in the general's and the president's ears with a back-translation into Mallor's ears. "This is the ship's computer speaking in translator mode. 'Shift-ring' is a term I coined from two of your words to designate the ring shaped devices which we use to open wormholes from one position in the space-time continuum to another. The krane carrier had opened a wormhole and was passing a shift-ring over itself in order to jump to a new location when Exceltor successfully cut the ring and collapsed the wormhole. Collapsing a wormhole transects any objects within the shift-ring orifice and thus should have cut the enemy ship into two pieces. The rear segment would be left in its original orbit while the front segment would be where it had arrived at the other end of the jump."

"Was that big flash an explosion from it being cut in half?"

The ensign, having heard the computer's translation message seemed at last to comprehend his audience's lack of basis for understanding. The ensign said, "No sir. Opening a 10 meter wormhole to pass the carrier requires a huge amount of energy. About one per-cent of that power leaks away as light and other lower frequency radiation." He looked away to one of the holotanks, "We estimate the flash at one megawatt, indicating an attempted jump of approximately one light second's distance, perhaps to the other side of your world."

"Only ten meters in diameter? You told us the thing was 700 meters long!"

"That's correct. Energy requirements to open a wormhole vary as the square of the diameter of the hole. This makes it most efficient to build ships that are very long yet slender. Exceltor at 7.1 meters diameter, is barely wider than the 5.3 meter width of the bridge you see before you, but she's nearly 200 meters long."

"Wait a minute. You said that one megawatt flash represented one percent waste? You're claiming it took 100 megawatts of energy to jump to the other side of the planet?"

"Correct. Actually that is an incredibly small amount of energy to move such a large mass such a distance at near instantaneous speed." Even the translation managed to sound huffy. "Without Vinzearian physics it couldn't be done."

"How did you cut the shift-ring?"

"Captain Leis is brilliant! He had small weapon locating port-rings located on the surface of the krane carrier as soon as we found it. He had them set to automatically transfer in weapon-rings and destroy the shift-ring if the krane tried to move."

"Weapon locating port-rings?"

The ensign said, "Port-rings are small versions of the shift-rings that can be held open for observation. We call rings that are used to attack the enemy weapon-rings."

At the front of the bridge, the captain wasn't feeling brilliant, just incredibly lucky and still damned scared. He turned to Azimus. "Lieutenant, the locals aren't lighting *us* up with their radar are they?"

"No sir. With our shift-flash shielded by the moon I don't think they know we're here yet."

"OK team. Have we got sets of sensor-rings behind that moon and on the far side of P3 to pick up any incoming jumps?"

"Yes sir."

BRIDGE—KRANE DESTROYER ZOADEN—MARS ORBIT
1000 EST

Captain Quinjot read with dismay the three messages from Commander Kinjie on Xajion. The first detailed the arrival of the humans into a moon eclipsed location and Kinjie's intention to shift to the other side of P3 before he was detected. The second message was from a lieutenant in the rear half of Xajion—which had been left in its original location by the collapsed jump—who still had locator ports extant in Zoaden's message bay. The sniveling spawn of a DNA oiton was pitifully begging for rescue. After some time for the front half of Xajion to extrude an antenna through a small port near Mars, a third terse message arrived from Xajion's bridge. "Xajion destroyed. Captain Jenkoit on the Yaitan is now in temporary command of the task force. Destruction of human cruiser paramount. Detail one rescue port to locate the Xajion bow fragment which is now in low P3 orbit opposite moon, approximate location data to follow."

Quinjot's cilia drooped and then commenced the jerky movements of a true fury. Jenkoit in command! Had Kinjie forgotten that Quinjot was senior? No! Kinjie had always favored that DNA based spawn of a suckerfish! Now he'd jumped Quinjot's seniority to put Jenkoit in command. Hah, Quinjot thought, Jenkoit will fall on his face like any other officer who won his position through influence rather than ability.

The angry buzzing of another red message light caught his attention. From Jenkoit of course. Quinjot was assigned to jump his ship Zoaden to a high P3 orbit. Of course! That placed him where the human ship was probably bound *and* might already be able to see. Jenkoit, like the coward he was, had placed Quinjot in the gravest danger. *And*, Jenkoit assigned Quinjot to locate the Xajion fragment and establish a rescue port which would pick up Kinjie. *Of course*, Jenkoit didn't want Kinjie on *his* ship!

Quinjot issued his own orders. First they would jump to as low a P3 orbit as could *possibly* be construed to follow the order to "jump to a high orbit." Second he assigned Quac, a chronic bumbler, to locate the Xajion fragment. If anyone could screw it up it would be Quac. Further orders located observation ports to be set up behind the moon and on the opposite side of the planet.

BRIDGE—KRANE DESTROYER YAITAN—VENUS ORBIT
1000 EST

Captain Jenkoit's mind quivered over the implications. *He* was now the mission commander. There would be tremendous potential for promotion if he were able to defeat the enemy that had just successfully dispatched Kinjie. Especially when Jenkoit brought a system this rich into the krane fold. Unfortunately, knowing Captain Quinjot, that excretory orifice would be seizing every opportunity to stab Jenkoit in the back over this "out of rank" promotion. Jenkoit would have to manage Quinjot in such a manner that the other captain couldn't hurt Jenkoit's plan without *directly* disobeying commands.

Quinjot had, no doubt, already located a jump into a lower orbit than Jenkoit had implied in his orders, but that was OK. Jenkoit also expected Quinjot to make an ineffective effort to establish a rescue port on the damaged carrier, Xajion. But, Jenkoit didn't really want Commander Kinjie back on the scene either. For Jenkoit's own destroyer Yaitan, he plotted a moon eclipsed transfer, but, not into an orbit. Instead Yaitan would come out on a "bounce" vector that launched it directly up from the surface of the moon at a velocity that would give him several hours before he had to jump again. The second jump would still be eclipsed; the only problem would be the fact that he *must* lose any located ports in four to five hours when the bounce came to an end.

The two krane destroyers exchanged message capsules with best possible descriptions of their upcoming jumps in order to enable rapid

64

communication-port linkup post jump and then they jumped almost simultaneously.

"Azimus, have you located the jumped fragment of the carrier yet?"

"No sir. Our observation port was pretty far from the arrival site and I haven't been able to massage a vector out of the record. I'm still driving some ports around trying to catch a visual, but I'm up to a pretty big search pattern by now."

"Snellen. What about the local message traffic? Did the locals on the planet pick up this jump too?"

"No sir. But you wouldn't expect the ordinary news services to be aware of a one megawatt jump-flash on the day side of a planet and governmental communications are hard to tap into."

The president spoke up. "Captain Leis. We might be able to help if…"

Azimus interrupted. "Captain! A 10 megawatt jump-flash, behind the planet! A 5 megawatt behind the moon. Probably destroyers incoming from somewhere else in the system. The 10 megawatt might be a cruiser depending on distance."

"You going to be able to pick them up?"

"Working on it sir."

"Captain Leis." The president spoke again. "Would it help if we tried to light them up with radar again?"

"It could if you can point your radar in the right direction. Snellen. Establish the president a comm link."

"*No Captain*, I must go back *myself*. In the first place, they'd better not take orders from me while I'm in your power. In the second, it's my *job* to be back there in the White House!"

65

"You're correct sir. Snellen, you and Gunny arrange a transfer back to the White House for the president and his assistant, then set up a comm link."

"Mr. President, I should stay here as liaison." The general leaned in close to his president. "Sir, if I'm under duress I'll stutter when I contact you." The minuscule "microphone port" that the computer was maintaining by the general's head picked up the whisper, but the word "stutter" was outside its current English vocabulary.

GUNNERY ROOM—HUMANIFORM CRUISER
EXCELTOR—COMETARY EARTH ORBIT
1020 EST

Nedcam looked up from his perusal of the investigation team's antics in the White House. Lt. Snellen had come in to say that she had the president in the transfer chamber and was decompressing it at the maximum safe rate to avoid the bends. She said, "Locate a suitable shift location for back-transfer of the president."

From the transfer room where he was looking at a mirrored image of Nedcam's screen showing the situation room, the president asked "Why not right into the middle of the room there?"

"Well sir, the shift-flash can be painful, if not damaging, to the eyes," Nedcam said. "When we were picking you up we had to wait quite a while for everyone to look away at one of your computer screens. We can have a safe transfer pretty much whenever we want if we just swing over into the hallway."

Rayland stopped cracking his jaw to ask, "Why aren't they noticing the light from the wormhole' we're looking through?"

"Sir, this wormhole is only one millimeter in diameter. Light emission varies by the square of the size and linearly with the distance of a wormhole. With this tiny wormhole, where we're only squaring one millimeter and bridging less than a light second's distance, it's emitting less than a hundredth of a watt—essentially unnoticeable."

When the decompression algorithm thought it was nearly safe, Lt. Snellen asked the president to stand on a pedestal in the center of a one meter ring and reminded him to keep his hands away from the metal rails the ring rode on. "Pull yourself in, open your mouth wide and close your eyes sir, you don't want the ring to touch you on its way up." No sooner than he had his hands all the way down at his sides there was a flash of light sensed right through his eyelids and gravity suddenly went up while air pressure dropped a little more. Because the pressure differential hadn't completely equalized, air whooshed out of his open mouth and his ears began to hurt again.

Rayland resumed cracking his jaw.

WHITE HOUSE SITUATION ROOM
1045 EST

A loud "foomp" in the corridor signaled the arrival of the president. The light flash reflected into the room and the air blown through the transfer-ring pushed the door shut. When the president pulled the door open a second later, still cracking his ears, he found himself staring into the barrels of several weapons.

"Jeez sir, what *happened* to you?"

"I'll explain in a minute, *but, we - are - now - at - war.* I want you to begin assembling the cabinet and the Joint Chiefs, NOW!"

The president heard in his earbud a tiny voice with Lt. Snellen's computer translation tonality. "Mr. President, you may speak to us on the ship at any time. I'm decompressing now so in another 20 minutes, if you feel it would be helpful to have a representative from Exceltor, I'll be available to transfer down to act as liaison. I'll have to wear an oxygen mask though."

BRIDGE—KRANE FLAGSHIP—LIGHT CARRIER
XAJION—BOW FRAGMENT—EARTH ORBIT
1050 EST

Commander Kinjie stood at the center of a turbulent boil of activity. He had suppressed outward signs of glee when Quell proved to be completely unarousable. He'd expressionlessly ordered the diplomat moved to his cabin. He'd pondered for a moment the fact that a similarly injured human would have had someone trying to repair him. *Thank the Mother the kranes don't do anything like that,* he thought.

Kinjie's heads darted back and forth as he barked orders to his remaining functional crew members. For a while he'd hoped that this fragment of Light Carrier Xajion might still fight. It had the bridge and the main ship shift-rings, as well as one set of accumulators and a single gunnery room with its weapon-rings. All the flickership bays had been lost with the stern of the ship, but he'd hoped this fragment might still carry on the war. Then had come the report that the accumulators had been holed by a star-port before the transfer wormhole collapsed. The Mother must have been with them since the accumulators hadn't blown, but they wouldn't hold a significant charge either. This fragment of the carrier wasn't going to shift or even open a significant weapon-ring until it got new accumulators. For now he was trying to get the wobble taken off the bow fragment with the few operational thrusters they had left. He had his navigation team trying to get a fix on their position. He'd also ordered navigation to figure out whether their orbit was stable, and started silently cursing

Jenkoit and Quinjot for not yet establishing a rescue shift-ring and getting him the hell *out* of here.

GUNROOM—KRANE DESTROYER ZOADEN—
EARTH ORBIT
1055 EST

Quac ventilated rapidly, but his nostril continued to show his agitation by producing fetid exhalations. After his foul-up on their last mission he was amazed that the captain had chosen him for the difficult and important task of establishing the rescue port to Xajion. Alternately his cilia drooped with his dismay regarding the likelihood of his success and stood on end with his relief over being chosen to find the bow fragment, surely a sign he'd regained respect somehow. The fragment was somewhere over the sunward side of the planet, but its altitude and orbit were only approximately known from the intended jump target that Xajion had communicated prior to jumping.

After the transected jump, Xajion had been unable to get a navigational fix on its own location with the stars rolling wildly about the tumbling ship fragment. Xajion's comm officer had extruded a radio antenna through a port in high P3 orbit so he could communicate with Zoaden, but it wouldn't do any good until Xajion figured out its own location. Besides, the humaniforms would soon track down Xajion's ported antenna and destroy it.

And, of course the Xajion fragment remained stealthy in order to keep the humaniforms from finding it, but that stealthed it against Quac's efforts too. *What was that glint? Could it be off the cut surface of Xajion?* Quac drove his port towards it. *No, it was just another one of those damn humaniforms' innumerable satellites.*

69

General Price leaned over to the ensign. "Mallor, are we under way yet?"

Mallor gave him a confused look, "Under way to where, sir?"

"To find these krane and try to fight them!"

"Oh, no sir. We can find them from here, sir. But if *we* move, they'll know where we are from the light of our shift-flash."

"So how *are* you finding them?"

"The gunnery room had ports open on the other sides of your planet and your moon when the krane jumped in. The gunners will be trying to chase the krane down with their location ports. Unfortunately, it can be pretty hard to catch a ship that jumps in with a high velocity at a significant distance from your ports. And, you can guarantee a warship jumping into a hostile situation is going to come in with a high velocity."

"Why? Don't the ports accelerate well?"

"They accelerate well, but when the krane jumped in we were using wide angle lenses to be sure to see the jump. Magnification is extremely low at a wide angle so telling what vector and velocity the incoming destroyers had is difficult. So we move ports to the area and start looking off on likely vectors at higher magnifications, but with their stealthing, ships can be pretty hard to see."

"So why don't you light them up with radar?"

"Takes a *big* port to extrude the kind of antenna that can emit and receive back useful data. Besides once the antenna starts to radiate, it's easy to find and blow away."

"Reminds me of submarine warfare. They're always sneaking around, hoping the *other* guy'll make mistakes. Can you take me down to this 'gunnery room'?"

"I'll ask sir. What are submarines?"

GUNNERY ROOM—HUMANIFORM CRUISER
EXCELTOR—COMETARY EARTH ORBIT
1105 EST

Mallor took General Price past the transport room with the rings on the floor where the general and the president had arrived. The gunnery room proved to be next to it. The gunnery room was another long narrow room filled with holocubes similar to the bridge, but these cubes displayed enhanced real images rather than the prevalent "computer simulation" type of images he had seen on the bridge. Several officers were gathered in front of a cube which was displaying a multicolored cylinder. Mallon said quietly, "That's the stern fragment of the krane carrier. The dark red areas are hotter on infrared. The warm areas you see represent the accumulator banks where they store energy." As they watched, the image zoomed in on one of the red spots and blanked for a second. A crackling boom came from a large cylinder at the back end of the room. The hair rose on the back of the general's neck at a sense of tremendous energy release. The image then zoomed back to show the red spot flaring and spewing violet streaks.

"What the hell are they doing Mallon?"

"They transferred a small port on the surface of the stern fragment to the star-port in that cylinder at the back of the room and blew a hole in the accumulator bank."

"My god! On Earth we don't keep shooting after we've blown a ship in half! We consider it gentlemanly to *help* the survivors after the battle is over."

Mallon shrugged, "We *are* being gentlemanly to our way of thinking. I'm afraid that stern fragment is still a

71

threat. It contains their flickerships and gunnery rooms. We're just blowing their energy accumulator banks with small star-ports. That way they can't open large ports to run their weapons. We *could* fry the whole fragment you know."

"Star-ports?"

"That's what we call our main weapons. Essentially they consist of two ports that are joined surface to surface so that there's only a small, heavily-armored, highly-reflective, supercooled area between them that's exposed to our location here. We locate one port on the enemy ship and the other we open into the photosphere of the nearest star. The end of the port that's in the star is almost immediately destroyed, but not before enough stellar material and radiation blows through to do significant damage to the target." The general heard a muffled "kerchunk" similar to a bolt being thrown home on a large gun. Mallon said, "That sound was a new star-port ring-pair being loaded into the cylinder over there. The cylinder itself is made of a superalloy armor to protect us in case of accidental ring blowout."

"How do you know that the krane don't have a port just outside our hull getting ready to blow a hole in *us*?"

"Unfortunately, we don't. Of course we have observation ports on the hull watching for the approach of such locator ports, but a small locator port just doesn't put out enough light to be easily seen. We just have to hope that we 'stealth' better than they do."

WHITE HOUSE—WASHINGTON DC
1105 EST

The group of his staff that surrounded President Rayland stared at him wide eyed. After a moment, the Chairman of the Joint Chiefs said, "Mr. President, let's get this straight. You were abducted by skinny humans. They told you that there were green skinned monsters out there trying to kill everyone on this planet. Now you're back and you want us to search near space with radar, looking for UFOs?"

The president stared at the chairman, slowly becoming aware of just how implausible his story sounded. His mind sifted for known facts. Drawing himself up, he said with some irritation, "*Not* green skinned… Admiral lets go over the objective data: One. There was some kind of large, but very dim, radar shadow in Earth orbit. Two. It was first noted after emitting so much light it was observed by tens of thousands of casual observers at two o'clock this morning. Three. A little over an hour ago it again emitted a lot of light. Four. It is now much smaller and is quite hot in several places as if some sections may have been damaged or burned. Five. A little more than an hour and a half ago I and General Price were abducted from here in association with a bright flash of light. I alone was returned unharmed, in another flash of light, just minutes ago. Now, I've explained what I've been led to believe plausibly explains all these events. This 'Humaniform Federation' is proposing to help us, if they can, for the price of an asteroid that we have no use for, and that they could easily just steal from us, if they wanted. Providing us help appears to put them in grave danger as Exceltor is significantly outmatched by its opponents. I *believe* that I've been told the truth and that we have *little* to lose by using our radar installations to try to light up the krane warships. If you have an alternate explanation of these events and can recommend a more reasonable course of action, then *I'm* all ears."

The president's words were delivered with the full force of his considerable personal charisma. As the room turned back to the Admiral, more than one of the individuals present were reflecting on the motto affixed to the front of the president's desk, "Don't bitch, don't dither, get it done."

The Admiral stared at the president for a minute, surprisingly no one else tried to get a word into the pause. "I don't know Fred. I just can't get myself around the implausibility of the whole thing. I have a sinking feeling that we're missing something."

"We might be, John, we might be. I, however, am unable to see how searching space for more of these ships will hurt us, other than wasting some time and money. *I* think it's time to fish or cut bait."

"Yes sir."

"If we're agreed then?" Nods around the room. "I'll ask Exceltor to give us their coordinates so that we won't accidentally irradiate them."

GUNNERY ROOM—HUMANIFORM CRUISER
EXCELTOR—COMETARY EARTH ORBIT
1230 EST

Nedcam turned to address the crew in the gunnery room. "OK team, it looks like some of the people down on P3 are going to help us by sweeping the areas where we think the krane might be with the microwave radiation that they call radar. They are not *supposed* to sweep our area. If they do we're in trouble because we reflect their radars' wavelengths a *lot* better than the krane. Considering the quality of the krane stealthing in the microwave range, for this to do us much good, we're going to need some antennas out there to pick up reflections. They'll be radiating large areas, therefore they won't light 'em up the way they did the carrier when they focused in on it. We'd need some luck to pick up a weak, sweep reflection with our shipboard antenna. We've only got four microwave type antennas in stores, but we're going to pop three of them out with a *bunch* of false port openings to try to keep the krane from recognizing and destroying the ones we care about."

General Price watched as the gun room crew wrestled a bulky antenna into an airlock. While they were bringing the antenna in, there were repeated thrumming booms coming from the airlock chamber which Mallon told him were "false port openings" designed to get the krane tired of trying to chase down every port they opened in near space. The actual loading of the antenna into the chamber to dump it through the port was a frenzied operation in order to send it through without a longer delay than the other port openings. Irregular timing would allow that port to be characterized as "special" by the krane. Once they'd sent the antenna through, they minimized the size of the port and brought the leads to the antenna out through the small port that remained. The leads and port were carried over and hooked into a holocube while another antenna was being prepared so it could be "popped out" as well. Shortly thereafter the holocube began to identify and display vectors to an amazing number of objects that were reflecting Earth's radar emissions.

The reflections mostly represented Earth's satellites and satellite fragments that were getting pinged by the radar sweeps. Because the people on Exceltor had no way of knowing when and where a signal that bounced off the space junk had been initially radiated, they didn't know its distance from the antenna, only its vector. After the second antenna had been deployed the two antennas triangulated, as well as noting the time difference it took a pulse to arrive at first one, then the other antenna. With this data, the holocube switched to displaying locations rather than vectors

BRIDGE—KRANE DESTROYER ZOADEN—EARTH ORBIT

Quinjot's cilia quivered as he pondered this new development. Exceltor had been opening two meter ports every 130 seconds all over near space. At 4 megawatts a pop, they were putting a fair amount of energy into this effort, but after looking down the vectors to a randomly chosen twenty and finding nothing, he was beginning to think that Exceltor must be doing it just to distract the kranes. Or perhaps they were temporary passive imaging portals? Open, get a snapshot, close and analyze.

A new report grabbed his attention. A lot more planet based sources were beginning to sweep space with beams of microwave radiation. Presumably they were trying to find out what was producing all the flashing lights in near space. Incredible luck! The wavelengths they were using were in a range where the kranes' stealthing was more effective than the humans'. Quinjot's initial impulse had been to shift the hell out of there before he was caught like he suspected Xajion had been, however, he was now realizing that this represented an incredible stroke of good fortune. If one of those beams swept Exceltor it would light up like an onmibull, whereas Zoaden would be hard to see without big antennas.

He decided to gut it out. "Rotan, deploy our own microwave antennas and see if we can pick up a ping off that humaniform ship. Then calculate the minimum size antenna ports we'd need to pick up a humaniform cruiser based on the strength of those microwave sweeps and open a couple on the other side of this damned planet." *Should I let Jenkoit know what's going on?* Quinjot wondered. *No!* he decided, *Let the scum sucker figure* something *out for himself.*

BRIDGE—KRANE FLAGSHIP—LIGHT CARRIER XAJION—BOW FRAGMENT—EARTH ORBIT

Commander Kinjie was fuming. He knew that a destroyer, either Zoaden or Yaitan, had shifted into an orbit lower than Xajion's because his navigation team had picked up the flash *despite* the severe damage to his fragment of a ship. The only port making equipment he had in this miserable fragment of a ship was the communications setup at the back of the bridge. The ports they'd been using to communicate with Yaitan and Zoaden in their P2 and P4 orbits just after the Xajion had been stricken. Gueel had been unable to find whichever ship had shifted in below Xajion using the comm ports without having the precision data they'd used to locate Yaitan and Zoaden in their previous orbits. However, Xajion had sent the other two ships some information on Xajion's current location in the message where Kinjie had transferred command to Jenkoit on Yaitan. *Any cretin with a full complement of search ports should have been able to find Xajion with that data by now!* Kinjie was getting a sinking feeling that giving command to the more competent, but more junior Jenkoit was the source of this problem. He doubted that a peeved Quinjot was *refusing* to search for Xajion, but the arrogant fool was just the type to assign one or two of his less qualified technicians to the task.

Even worse, two meter ports had been opening all over creation and now planet-based units were sweeping the area with microwave frequencies. That damned Humaniform Federation *must* have had prior contact with this Mother-forsaken planet. Duot had finally gotten up the courage to tell Kinjie that they had been heavily irradiated by multiple planet-based sources of microwave just prior to their jump. No wonder Exceltor had found them so quickly. They must've just called their buddies on the planet, who'd seen Xajion's in-shift flash, and asked them to radiate the whole area with those big, crude, planet-based antennas. *Now* they were having them sweep around to try to find Zoaden and Yaitan the same way. Exceltor had probably popped some 10 meter "blossom" antennas out through some of those 2 meter ports. Quinjot, that offspring of a DNA fertilized egg, probably hadn't figured any of this out yet and, since he hadn't established contact, couldn't be told! Cilia wilting, Commander Kinjie spoke, "Fotayl, have you been able to rig the radio to broadcast on an antenna extruded through that damn comm port yet?"

"No sir."

"How much longer?"

"Fifteen or twenty more minutes, sir.

"Too slow. Coded radio message to Zoaden and Yaitan, direct from our shipboard antennas. 'Suspect that planet-based microwave radiators are in communication with Exceltor, therefore they will *not* sweep Exceltor for you. Recommend that you destroy radiators immediately. If you *are* swept by their radar, assume that Exceltor will have picked you up on blossom antennas that they extruded through some of those 2 meter ports. Jump *immediately* to safety. Quinjot, if, as I suspect, you have assigned your least-qualified port technicians to find and establish the rescue port to this fragment of Xajion, then I recommend your court martial for dereliction of duty *if* Zoaden ever successfully returns to Krane. I expect the humaniforms will home in on this radio message and destroy this fragment of Xajion in a few more minutes. Good hunting to you."

BRIDGE—HUMANIFORM CRUISER EXCELTOR—
COMETARY EARTH ORBIT
1402 EST

Lt. Snellen turned abruptly in her chair, "Captain! Krane-type radio broadcast, opposite side of P3!

Coded, should take ten to twenty minutes to break the code. The broadcast antenna was not within line of site for Exceltor, but one of our blossom antennas has a directional fix and approximate vector."

"Pass it to the gunnery room and have them check it out. I assume it came from a ported antenna from the bow fragment of that carrier. They probably can't get back in direct port communication with the destroyers. Must be in pretty bad shape."

Azimus exclaimed, "Whoa! Captain, one of the dirtside microwave radar antennas just swept that region and it looks like the bow fragment is actually *at* that location. They *must* be in bad shape if they can't even port an antenna!"

"Have gunnery assign two ports to finish disabling the bow fragment, but keep everyone else on the search for those destroyers."

BRIDGE—KRANE DESTROYER ZOADEN—EARTH ORBIT
1404 EST

With dismay Quinjot read and reread the message from Quell. Mother's carapace! Now he *must somehow* find that DNA-based scum before the humaniform ship did, or at least cover his tracks.

"Kueck! Have you found Xajion's bow fragment yet?"

"Sir? You assigned Quac that task, sir. I'm looking for the humaniform ship, as I have been tasked, sir."

"I assigned who?"

"Quac, sir."

"I couldn't have. I specifically remember assigning you!"

"Sorry sir. We thought you said Quac. In any case he's just found the fragment sir. We homed him in on the radio broadcast, sir."

"For the Mother's sake get a port in there and rescue them!"

79

"Working sir."

"OK also assign three gunnery teams to destroy those planet-based microwave broadcasters."

Quinjot was nervously wondering whether he'd sounded sincere when he heard the words he dreaded.

"Sir, we've just been pinged by one of those planet-side microwave sweeps!"

*Damndamndamndamn, damn!* Quinjot's left head turned, then both began darting back and forth indecisively. "Give me a running count on the time since the ping! Prepare for emergency shift... back to P4! Is that rescue port working yet?"

"Opening now sir."

"Get them over here, NOW!" Quinjot turned his right head to check the running count. *Thirty seconds! How long would it take the humaniforms to track them down from that ping?* "Is that escape shift set up?"

"The shift-ring's already set up sir. We're locating the P4 shift. We had a getaway shift already set to the backside of P6 if you want it sir."

"Keep it! If I call shift and P4 isn't ready, go to P6. Observers, any sign of a targeting port vectoring in on us?"

"No sir."

"If you see one, don't report it, just call for emergency shift!" He thought uneasily about how slim the chance of seeing a targeting port actually was.

BRIDGE—HUMANIFORM CRUISER EXCELTOR—COMETARY EARTH ORBIT
1406 EST

"Captain, we think we have a ping on the destroyer behind P3!"

"Feed gunnery." The captain said. He murmured, "Gun room." Then, "Guns, rush multiple ports to the location of this ping that we're feeding you. They must know they've been pinged and will be pulling their antennas in preparation for jump. Blow holes in 'em as soon as the first ports get there; don't wait for other ports to arrive." He thought, *We can't possibly get many chances like this against these odds.*

"Working sir."

Captain Leis turned to Azimus. "What do you think's going on with the ship that jumped in behind the moon? None of our ports have caught a glimpse and the planet based radars have now swept the entire circumference. At the altitude they jumped in at, any sustainable orbit would have brought them out from behind the moon by now. You think they came out so fast that they're already beyond our sweep or did we just miss them because of their better stealthing?

A glazed look passed over Azimus' face as he rocked in his seat. "Don't think their stealthing is *that* good sir... I can back calculate from the reflection we just got off the other one though. I'll also calculate what their incoming velocity would have to have been to be beyond the first sweeps." His head tilted to an odd angle and he began murmuring to the computer.

GUNNERY ROOM—HUMANIFORM CRUISER
EXCELTOR—COMETARY EARTH ORBIT
1408 EST

The long narrow room hung thick with the odor of nervous sweat. General Price found himself pacing back and forth along the rows of "cubes," each with its own team of two to three operators. Price looked over their shoulders into the displays as if by staring harder he could somehow make an enemy ship appear in one of them. His skin crawled with the sensation that one of the enemy's locator ports was just outside the wall of the chamber getting ready to position a star-port and blow them all to hell.

Suddenly, with a quiver in his voice, one of the noncoms shouted to Nedcam. "Sarge, I've got 'em! I've got 'em!"

Nedcam bellowed. "Teams one, three, nine, and twenty two! Take splits from Delos! Put some holes in it! It's gonna jump!"

Price ran to where Delos sat at the number two cube. Delos' cube showed the long, thin "false color" image of one of these "wormhole ships" and he saw the ring at one end brightly sparkling. The two cubes next to Delos' immediately came alive with the same image and then began to diverge as their operators took the new ports that they had "located" on Delos' off at slightly different angles, though still rushing toward the ship. As the cubes' viewpoints rushed in close, loud booms repeatedly crashed through the room from the big cylinders in the back. The cubes' displays zoomed back and showed radical changes. The "ship" started to deform and violet "false color" sparks and plumes began spraying out into the surrounding space from several sections.

BRIDGE—KRANE DESTROYER YAITAN—EARTH ORBIT
1415 EST

"Captain, I think Zoaden's been hit! Their comm-port's just translocated violently!"

"What? The motherless scum hadn't shifted? Didn't they pick up Kinjie's message?" Jenkoit's cilia stood on end and his exhalations began to cloud up. What else could possibly go wrong? How could a single humaniform cruiser, *even* if aided by the retrogressed locals, possibly have destroyed a light carrier and now a destroyer in just a few hours? Sure, there was a lot of luck involved in wormhole warfare, but this was *beyond* belief! "Locate a rescue port on that comm-port and see if we can bring any of them out. How

82

much longer 'til we have to re-shift to keep from crashing back into this damned moon?"
"Four hundred seventy five seconds sir."
"Set the shift on automatic, to go at the last second."
"Do you still want a bounce-type vertical relaunch sir?"
"Yes! What'd you think, that we were going to run?"
Quietly, "No sir."

GUNNERY ROOM—KRANE DESTROYER
ZOADEN—EARTH ORBIT
1416 EST

Commander Kinjie lay stunned on his side, his left head-hand weaving drunkenly in the air and his right stretched out flaccid on the deck. His relieved joy when the rescue port had blinded everyone by opening in the front of Xajion's bridge had turned into dismay when, seconds after he ran through the port into Zoaden's gunnery transport room, the destroyer had been wracked with violent explosions. His carapace had slammed into a bulkhead with stunning force and now he was having great difficulty controlling his neuromuscular system. To his horror, it seemed that all three of his excretory orifices had spilled involuntarily. The slippery mess beneath him was contributing to his difficulty in getting his feet-claws back to supporting him.
A minute passed and Kinjie found his legs had regained sufficient control that he was able to rise unsteadily and begin moving up the passageway toward the bridge. Another clap of thunder rang through the ship. The artificial gravity suddenly went off. At first Kinjie was dismayed, but then realized wonderingly that much of the clumsy motor dysfunction he'd been struggling with had been weakness. Without gravity, he found he could propel

himself forward more easily, though reaching things to push off of remained difficult.

Kinjie realized that part of the reason he was traveling well was because he was being pulled along by a strong air current! There must be a hull breach near the bow! *Why didn't the bulkhead doors close?* he wondered. Then he realized, *Ach, the power cabling must be cut too!*

Kinjie's pressure suit began to activate, indicating that there'd been a significant pressure drop. He peered ahead into the bridge with his good left head-hand. The images coming from his right head-hand's eye cluster as it banged along flaccidly beside him kept distracting him. Zoaden's bridge was strewn with floating bodies and moaning victims. He noted, with the same satisfaction he'd felt over diplomat Quell's injury, that Captain Quinjot was one of the completely flaccid ones, drifting and slowly revolving near the ceiling, apparently dead. The bridge seemed to be losing air through multiple small holes, rather than one big one.

As Kinjie turned to look toward the comm-ports, a tremendous flash of light from the opening of Yaitan's rescue portal nearly blinded him. Recognizing it for what it was, Kinjie immediately launched himself toward it. The blast of wind blowing out of the rescue portal into the low pressure of Zoaden's bridge pushed him back. Kinjie caught himself on a desk and relaunched toward the portal, harder this time. The rescue port's airlock chamber was now nearly empty so the resistance of the air current had died down. Kinjie sailed through the rescue portal, only to crash agonizingly to the floor in the normal gravity field beyond the portal. *Mother! What a mess!*

A noncom lifted Kinjie in the necks of both of her head-hands and carried him to the lock as others scurried into Zoaden to search for other kranes to rescue. Kinjie's functioning left head-hand turned and maneuvered close to the ear on the noncom's right head where it was supporting the front of Kinjie's own carapace. "Take me to the bridge," he said, the sound coming out as a whispered croak.

Kinjie found himself lulled by the sound of the noncom's claws as they clattered down the long passageway toward the bridge. He was again strangely disturbed by the receding, rolling, out-of-focus view behind him that came from his flaccid right head-hand. With a supreme effort, he found that he could pull that head-hand around and get it looking forward. To his relief, the view from that eye cluster, though tilted and still out of focus, merged into the dominant picture from the left head-hand and even gave him some fuzzy sense of binocular depth.

Jenkoit was not sure whether he was dismayed or amused at the picture Commander Kinjie made as he was carried onto the bridge. He lay on a noncom's carapace, cradled by the noncom's necks. His left head-hand wove drunkenly in the air and the right head-hand lolled on his own carapace. When the noncom slid him off onto the floor it appeared for a minute that the commander might tip over onto the back of his carapace to lay helplessly with his legs waving in the air like some kind of bug. At the last moment the noncom caught and righted him, getting smeared grossly in the process by some of the yellowish circulatory fluid leaking from a crack on the right side of Kinjie's carapace. Jenkoit wondered for a moment whether Kinjie's injuries were permanent. Before he could speak however, multiple sensors on the bridge recorded Yaitan's shift-ring flash.

Kinjie's left neck became suddenly rigid at full extension and he managed to look imperious despite his drooping right head-hand. "Why are you shifting? You've lost the rescue port on Zoaden!"

"Yes sir," Jenkoit found himself responding before he remembered Kinjie had been seriously injured and didn't deserve such respect anymore. "We were in a bounce trajectory on the back side of their moon and had to shift before we struck."

"Where have we shifted to?"

"Sir, we re-bounced."

"You what?" Kinjie's voice was incredulous. "A bounce is *occasionally* a good trick. Once! Do you really think you are going to surprise someone as sharp as that captain on Exceltor twice with the *same* trick?!"

Jenkoit's heads lowered a fraction and his cilia developed a slight droop. He didn't respond. His crew looked on in amazement to see him dominated by an *injured* krane!

Kinjie turned on the bridge crew next, barking commands in the odd tone that his use of a single head-hand produced. "Get the crew working on an emergency reload for a new shift-ring! What the *space* are you looking at! Have you located the humaniform cruiser and you're just standing there with your mouths open waiting to tell me?"

"No sir," a chorus.

"Well then get *moving* for the *Mother's* sake! Have the gunroom detail someone to reestablish a rescue port on Zoaden. Also see if we can open a port on the stern fragment of Xajion. Maybe we can use some of its weaponry. Target a safety transfer behind P5. Target a maximum accumulator escape shift back toward Kaldon. Start destroying those ground based microwave antennas. How many shift-rings do we have left for this boat?"

"Five, sir."

"Mother's Mother! So, after we shift out of this damned bounce, we'll only have one shift to play with if we're to save three for an escape back to Kaldon?!"

"Yes sir," Jenkoit said weakly, feeling totally humiliated.

BRIDGE—HUMANIFORM CRUISER EXCELTOR—
COMETARY EARTH ORBIT
1421 EST

Azimus broke out of his reverie and became
motionless for a moment. "Sir, the numbers say that
the krane stealthing is not good enough for us to have
missed them coming out from behind the moon. They
may, of course, have had a high enough velocity for
us to have missed them, but a velocity that high would
not produce an orbit around either that moon or P3."
"So what do you think? Are they launched out from
behind that moon at a high velocity? Could they have
landed back there?"
"Sir, this is a *big* moon. Its gravity may be low but it's
still *way* too high to land a ship."
Suddenly the ensign working with Azimus shouted.
"Sir, double shift-flash behind that moon! Ring
diameters both about 6 meters, probable krane
destroyers. Flash brilliance low, they didn't come from
very far sir."
"How close?"
"No more than a few light seconds sir."
"What? Did anyone else pick up their origination
flash?" Leis looked around the bridge to see a lot of
shaking heads.
"They bounced!" Azimus leapt out of his own chair
and pumped a fist with his proclamation. "That's why
we didn't find them! The bastards bounced!"
"Could they have re-bounced?!" A dawning light of
amazement crossed the captain's face as he shouted,
"Get a vertical view on those last two shift-sites! If
they re-bounced, they're toast."

JOHNSON SPACE RADAR STATION—WHITE
SANDS, NEW MEXICO
1425 EST

Specialist Juan Gomez was about a mile away from the station on his way home when it happened. Because of all the excitement he'd stayed way past the end of his shift that morning. First they'd been called on to try to locate, resolve, and identify the object that had produced that big flash directly overhead at 0206 their time. He'd been outside on break to smoke a cigarette at the time and the flash had startled him. He'd been running back into the building within seconds, trying to get the attention of everyone for what he'd thought was an aircraft explosion. To his amazement over the next few hours it became obvious not only from their own radar, but on feeds from other sites, that the flash had come from orbit; had come from an impossibly large object; and had left the object intact. This morning another big flash and a series of smaller ones had obviously damaged the object. It was like there was some kind of space war going on up there! Then they'd been tasked to sweep near space for other such objects. In the excitement, he'd just kept staying there at work. At noon his supervisor had seen him and sent him home, "To get some sleep because they were surely going to need some fresh people tonight."
He initially thought the blinding flash in his rearview mirrors was brilliant sunlight off the windshield of a car right behind him. A microsecond later his mind caught up with the fact that the flash was *way* too bright *and* that he knew there wasn't a car behind him. He slewed off the road and looked back. "A-bomb," was all that went through his mind as he slashed the car back onto the road and began trying to put some distance between himself and the huge cloud of destruction back at the radar site. *What in God's name was going on!*

BRIDGE—KRANE DESTROYER YAITAN—EARTH ORBIT

1432 EST

Kinjie was now in Jenkoit's command saddle. Jenkoit skittering nervously about on the deckplates behind him, wondering in dismay how he had let an *invalid* usurp command of *his* ship, *and* amazed at Kinjie's sheer level of dominance in this bizarre situation. In an odd voice, for his right head-hand, though functioning better, continued to slur his speech, Kinjie barked, "Is the ship's shift-ring loaded yet?"
"Yes sir."
"Did you successfully disable the superconduction on its outer half?"
"Yes sir."
"Okay everyone, we're making a shift to the backside of P5 and this disabled shift-ring is gonna make it radiate like we're shifting several light months... *if* it lasts long enough for us to complete our transit. May the Mother bless us all. Begin shift."

BRIDGE—HUMANIFORM CRUISER EXCELTOR—
COMETARY EARTH ORBIT
1430 EST

Azimus spun in his seat, "Captain! I've found them! They did re-bounce! I sent a viewport to the site of their last shift-flash, looked straight up, and there they were! I'm feeding the gunroom now. We might get *another* one!"
Leis felt his pulse hammering. How could they be so lucky? There *must* be something about to go wrong. He must have overlooked something! He found himself nervously rubbing his bald pate beneath his comm ring. "'Puter, gunroom... Guns, it looks like a destroyer from its shift-flash, blow it away as soon as you possibly can! This is no time for finesse, go for it now, now, now!" Leis found himself fiercely gripping

his seat arms as if the force of his hands could somehow hurry the ports along.

Suddenly Azimus shouted, "They're shifting! They're shifting! Dammit! They shifted! Looks like a big shift too, way out of the system. Dammit! We didn't even scratch 'em."

Many of the crew on the bridge were looking around wildly, as if they could locate the enemy with their eyes. Leis found himself doing the same thing. He took a deep breath, blew it out slowly and then, surprised himself with the apparent calm in his voice as he said, "'Puter, all hands... OK crew, we did *great*, we hurt a light carrier and a destroyer, we didn't get hurt ourselves, and we ran another destroyer out of the system. That's good work, but we can't breathe the big sigh of relief yet. They might have another destroyer or even a cruiser in system. They *might* jump right back. We need to keep alert, do our level best to be sure this system is really clear, and get organized to jump out and get some help!"

Leis turned, "Azimus. Get your team organized. Tetrahedral viewports on every planet in this system. I don't want them sneaking back in and surprising us the way we surprised them."

"Swayze. Start plotting a jump back home. While we're waiting, fire off a bunch of trial jump locator ports and hope you hit one *really* close to Avajan."

"'Puter connect me to Snellen... Snellen! How goes it down there? Have you set us up a diplomatic team yet? We might need to make a fast run to Avajan."

Snellen's voice sounded a little odd in the mask she wore down on P3, nonetheless, Leis could hear a tone of frustrated amusement. "Captain, they're still working on radiating space with their radars. Let me tell them that you won the battle for now. *Then* I'll start talking to them about a diplomatic team."

SITUATION ROOM—WHITE HOUSE

Speaking to his Chief of Staff, President Rayland said, "Get me a list of foreign ambassadors who *are* here in town. Tell the Secretary of State we need her here immediately." President Rayland turned to the Chairman of the Joint Chiefs, "Admiral, I'd like you to find the most tech savvy upper-level general or admiral you have and send him with our diplomatic team. Oh, and General Price says we should assign a hot-shot submarine captain to the team too." He looked at Lt. Snellen, "We'll have you a diplomatic team here in the next few hours." He lifted his chin interrogatively, "Now, what the hell happened to our three radar installations?"

"I can't, of course, be sure Mr. President. From what I've heard of the reports you've received, it would appear that the one in New Mexico was destroyed by a star-port. The other two sound like 'gas giant dumps.'"

"Good Lord, what in the devil's name is a 'gas giant dump'?"

"If you open one end of a double port deep into the atmosphere of a gas giant such as your 5$^{th}$ planet and the other end opens at a target site, high pressure atmospheric gases pour through. The gases are toxic, rapidly expanding due to their pressure, cold and, usually quite flammable in an oxygen atmosphere. Gas giant dumps can be nearly as destructive as a star-port and often the rings for the double port are quite salvageable afterwards, unlike the complete destruction of the rings that occurs when you use a star-port."

"Damn..." President Rayland said, trailing off with a thoughtful expression on his face. He looked back at Snellen, "But, you say you've beaten the krane?" Snellen looked uneasy, "We think and hope so, Mr. President. We can't be sure."

The president gave her an incredulous look, "What do you mean, 'you can't be sure'? I thought you'd nearly destroyed two of their ships and the other one turned tail and ran?"

Snellen waggled her head from side to side, the equivalent of a shrug on her home world. "It's *very* easy to hide in deep space, Mr. President. The kranes could have had more than the three ships we know about in your solar system. We *know* we've cut their light carrier in half. We're *sure* we've severely damaged one of their destroyers. The other destroyer made a shift jump which emitted a very bright flash suggesting that it jumped all the way out of your system…" she hesitated, "but it hasn't been damaged. It could just jump back."

President Rayland stared at her for a minute, "Or, couldn't it be on its way back home to get reinforcements?"

Snellen sighed, "Yes it could. So, Captain Leis has an extremely difficult decision in front of him."

Rayland's eyes narrowed, "What decision?"

She waggled her head again, "Stay here to try to protect you if that destroyer returns… or, go for reinforcements." She glanced away, then turned back to look the President in the eye. "He's *got* to do one or the other… but either decision could doom every living thing on your planet."

A single tear tracked down her cheek.

**The End**

Inspired (distantly) by the Hunt for Red October

## MACOS

The night was ill-lit by a sliver of moon. The moon itself lay partially obscured by high, drifting cirrus clouds. The air was beginning to cool, but the earth remained hot from a scalding summer day. "It's a great night for this," Steb puffed as the three young men struggled up the embankment.

"You've got to be kidding!" Jos, as usual, disapproved. "*Any* night is an insane night for this kind of madness! I can't believe you two idiots talked me into this! Why can't we stick to the little stuff like we've been doing? Flat tires and sugared tanks cause the Stossa plenty of trouble without getting us into things they'd *kill* us for!"

Nigel turned. "Hey Jos, cool down. We're not gonna get caught, but you can go on home if you want. Steb and I can do this by ourselves."

"Sure, you and the 'war hero's' nephew. Of course. *You* can do anything by yourselves," Jos muttered.

Steb stopped short of the top and shrugged out of his pack. He was thinking that Nigel's words "Steb and I" had effectively cornered him with no way to agree with Jos's assertion that this mission *was* a little bit too dangerous. Steb used his boot to kick a small depression for the heavy bucket full of icy water that he and Nigel had been carrying.

While Nigel and Jos continued to argue, Steb shucked his slender frame out of his clothes, extracted his wire cutters and lighter, then dropped the clothes into the bucket of cold water. Pulling on a stocking cap soaked in the ice water made him wish he hadn't cut his hair so short. He picked up their low light goggles and crawled to the top of the embankment. Peering over the edge, he searched for and found the infrared motion sensors just inside the fence and picked a spot midway between them. With a grimace he skidded back, gave the goggles to Nigel and pulled on his icy cold shirt and pants. Then he crawled forward over the warm ground to carefully cut a window in the chain link fence.

Jos, apparently giving up the argument, but unable to bring himself to "weenie out," also put his clothes in the bucket. He then dragged his equipment twenty feet to the left to set up the six inch pipe that was their "mortar." The bottom had been capped and a small hole drilled in it. Two empty cans cut into skeletons kept the bottom 10 inches of the pipe open. The top part of the pipe had been lined and wadded with paper. Hundreds of small glass vials found behind the hospital had been filled with fuel, plugged with rag wicks to make little Molotov cocktails, and stacked into the top end of the pipe. Jos squirted more of the volatile fuel through the hole and onto the rag in the bottom section so that the skeletonized can would fill with explosive vapor. Then he inserted the remote controlled wires into the hole that were supposed to spark and fire off the mortar. He stretched out the antenna wire and threw one end of it up onto a bush.

Nigel put on his low light goggles and laid out the rest of their equipment. He checked the pressure in their alcohol canisters and attached them to the tubing that had been painstakingly sewn into their clothing.

Slowly, Nigel moved up to look over the edge. He used his hand to shade his low light goggles from the guard shack's bright lights and carefully surveyed the rest of the grounds. *Ah!* There was actually a guard out patrolling. A hand held up told Steb and Jos to wait. When the guard started to wend his way back to the shack, Nigel scrambled back down to fill the others in on the situation.

As they forced their bodies into the ice cold clothing, Nigel restrained his chattering teeth and described the layout of the compound. As they'd hoped, the tanks and armored personnel carriers were closer to the barracks; the general transport vehicles were distributed around the periphery.

A few seconds after the guard got back to the shack, they pulled the icy stocking caps over their heads. Freshly doused with the remains of the cold water from the bucket the three young men moved down the hill and climbed through the hole in the fence one at a time and walked slowly out amongst the vehicles. As they had hoped, midway between detectors, their cold images failed to set off the infrared motion recognition system.

They gathered at the first transport and Nigel climbed under the fuel tank. He placed his triflanged punch near the corner to prevent a boom from impact on a flat surface. Nigel wrapped the point of the awl with a piece of towel to dampen the sound, and with a sharp blow to the base, punched a hole in the tank with only a muffled thump. He removed the punch but to his dismay only a slow dribble began from the hole. However, with another blow and a wiggle, fuel began to stream out at a satisfactory rate. Each of the three filled a bottle with fuel, capped it and put it in a pocket. They spread out and soon fell into a routine, crawling from truck to truck, punching holes while puddles of fuel slowly grew under the vehicles.

In the guard shack Yasso nervously tugged at his thin, wiry beard. He was a small man of sudden quick movements. He'd been nicknamed "Bug" because of these, insect-like movements. He stepped to the open window and looked out, then cocked his head to one side. Finally he turned to Moman. "Do you hear thumping noises?"

"Dammit Bug! You hear those sounds every night, when it gets colder, the trucks settle." Moman scratched at his crotch and thought, *Yasso's such a damned weenie, worry, worry, worry!*

"But there are more tonight!"

Moman waved his hand and turned back to his magazine.

Yasso turned to the door. "I'm going out for a look around." He stepped out and pulled on his low-light goggles. Then he swore in a clipped fashion as they whited out with light from the nearby window. He flipped the goggles to infrared and began surveying the compound.

When the door of the shack opened Nigel was rounding the front of a truck and froze in his crouched position. He reached slowly for his alcohol valve and flipped it open, gritting his teeth at the shock of cold fluid spraying into his clothing.

Yasso halted abruptly. There was a warm object at the front corner of one of the trucks! His brow furrowed as he stared at it, but it slowly faded away to a few small splotches. He stepped away from the shack to use his goggles on the low light setting.

When Nigel saw the guard's head bob down to check the guard shack's steps before descending, he darted back behind the truck. He dropped to the ground and crawled under the truck to look for the guard's feet. Nigel still had on his low-light goggles, but the damn things were useless since he was looking toward the lighted shack.

He lifted the goggles. *There!* He could see the guard's boots outlined in the light from one of the windows. They stood motionlessly for a while, then began to walk his way.

Nigel felt his pulse booming as his body demanded that he do something—anything! The excitement and the cold from the rapidly evaporating alcohol made it so he had to clench his teeth to keep them from chattering. With dismay he realized that the boots were fading from view as the guard got further from the lighted shack. He inched backward toward the far side of the truck.

He couldn't see the boots anymore! But, now he could hear their tread. They stopped and he could imagine their owner listening with his head cocked. For a moment, he was grateful that he had yet to puncture a fuel tank in this row of trucks. The wind was blowing away, so you couldn't smell the fuel spilling. Then, to his dismay he heard a ping and high pitched whine as the superconductors of the guard's kalsaw (Kinetic And Laser Superconducting Attack Weapon) charged. When the boots moved again, Nigel began to back out farther. He bumped his head and felt the padding of the strap from the low light goggles, forgotten on his head! Silently cursing himself, he pulled them down and saw the guard's boots at the back of the truck. Moving toward Nigel's own feet which were hanging out from under the truck's left rear corner! Nigel pulled his feet in and clutched his awl.

The damn guard stopped right beside his feet! *Did he see a scuff? Did he see my boot? Did he smell the fuel?*

The guard suddenly resumed his deliberate pace around and back toward the front of the truck. Once again he stopped... After an eternity, the guard slowly headed back to the shack.

Breathing a collective sigh of relief, the three young men resumed punching holes. Finishing the trucks, they reached the armored vehicles. The fuel tanks on the armored vehicles were fully proof against an awl, but the caps on the tanks were not proof against a few lumps of sugar. After sugaring the tanks, they snapped back the lids on the compartments full of charged superconductors that powered the tank's electrical weapons. Uncapping their bottles they dribbled the solvent fuel onto the plastic that insulated the superconductors.

And so it went for seven of the ten tanks and twelve of the armored personnel carriers.

Suddenly the guard shack door slammed open! Both guards appeared, pulling their goggles into place and trotting ten paces from the shack.

The Macos immediately opened their alcohol valves, but Nigel felt only a small trickle of the cold fluid! He'd used up almost the entire can in the previous episode. Fortunately he was on the far side of an APC.

The guards moved out into the lane between the nearest vehicles. Their goggles were on infrared, looking for the man-sized infrared blob that Yasso had seen through their open window a few seconds ago. Moman had already begun to berate "Bug" for wasting their time when Nigel became visible as a splotchy blob crouched behind an APC. Thumbing his kalsaw to laser/infrared he shouted, "Who goes there!" To his embarrassment his voice broke. "Who goes there!" he said again.

He brought his weapon to bear while thumbing it to infrared. The blob disappeared around the corner of the APC. Depressing the trigger, he began walking toward the APC while waving the kalsaw back and forth over the area where he had last seen the blob. Yasso, he noted with satisfaction, was moving toward the other side of the APC.

It was probably the Lieutenant running one of his surprise checks, Moman thought, but if so, the infrared codes on the Lt.'s helmet and uniform would keep the kalsaw from firing. He quickly rounded the corner and came face to face with the blob! The damn kalsaw didn't fire as he convulsively crushed the trigger. *Oh, it's Yasso!*

*Where'd the intruder go?!*

The two guards spun away from each other.

Steb saw the guards turn toward Nigel, shout and then move toward him as Nigel darted, first behind the APC, then under it. Steb stepped behind the tank he'd been working on. He pulled out the rag he had in his back pocket and jammed it into his bottle that was now only half filled with fuel. He frantically spun the wheel until his lighter flared. A second later the rag was on fire. He heaved the Molotov cocktail hard at a truck in the next row, but it struck the canvas side and fell to the dirt without breaking!

As Moman spun away from Yasso his kalsaw lased a burst of three! The target was a small hot object on the ground near a truck. He lifted his goggles to look at it in real light. It was a small torch wobbling across the ground! There were glowing laser burns in the dirt to either side of it, but the torch apparently hadn't been damaged by the beam that had hit it. Suddenly more fire blossomed at the end of the left laser burn where it went under the truck! In a flash, flames engulfed the whole truck! *Shit! How did that happen? The Lieutenant's gonna have my ass!*

Jos stabbed frantically at the remote control button for their "mortar." Why wasn't it working?! He ran for the fence to fire it manually.

Nigel lay under the APC waiting for them to decide to look under the truck. He pulled on his low lights so he could see where they were. The flames of

Steb's unexploded Molotov cocktail nearly blinded him, but before he could lift the goggles he heard the kalsaw lase and saw the flashes by the bottle. When he got the goggles off he saw that the whole truck was going up in flames! He scooted back out from under the APC. His foot struck something.

It was the guard's boot!

Yasso looked down from the burning truck when something struck his ankle. To his amazement, in the light of the burning vehicle he saw that he had been kicked by someone backing out from under the APC! Saboteurs! He noted with amazement that his kalsaw had lased as he swung it at the man, finger still crushing the trigger. The saboteur began to thrash wildly about on the ground! The damn kalsaw lased another burst and he absently took his finger off the trigger. The saboteur only quivered now.

With some pride, and also some dismay, Yasso thought, *I've killed someone!* He flipped on his helmet mike and shouted, "Saboteurs, saboteurs in the compound!"

Yasso ran around the APC to Moman who was dazedly watching the truck burn. Suddenly a flash of heat behind them signaled the explosion of another truck into flames. They spun towards the new fire and their kalsaws lased again, firing at the hot truck. *Shit!* Together they thumbed the kalsaws to manual. Suddenly two neighboring trucks burst into flames! *What the hell was going on? Trucks didn't burn that easily!*

*Did they?*

Steb ran behind the APC to where Nigel lay motionless. There was a smoking hole in the back of Nigel's head! A great dread gripped Steb, but gritted his teeth and turned Nigel over. He stared into lifeless eyes. *Damn! Damn, damndamndamn....*

The guards were coming back! Steb turned and ran. Fear ripped through him. His gut turned to ice and his rubbery legs seemed to be moving in slow motion. A distant part of him was embarrassed as he felt his bladder convulse and piss run down his leg, scalding hot in contrast to the recent freezing driblets of alcohol. He twisted around the corner of the APC and turned toward the fence. His vision tunneled down to the area just ahead of him, but he vaguely noted a laser burst to his right and then to his left. *They must be shooting on manual,* he thought, *either that or I just haven't felt the killing shots… yet.*

Yasso missed the second saboteur as he rounded the corner of the APC. He himself rounded the corner a second later and waved his kalsaw at the running figure outlined so well in the light from the burning trucks. Both laser bursts missed! *Damn! It's still on manual!* There weren't any fires that direction to distract the kalsaw! He flipped back to infrared and pulled the trigger, but in that moment a truck just to the left of the running figure burst into flames and the kalsaw burst went directly into it. He pulled the kalsaw to the right to get the burning truck out of its field, but the figure turned a corner and disappeared. *Shit!*

Jos scrabbled at the base of their "mortar." He pulled the useless "spark wire" out of the hole at the bottom and held his lighter to it. A thunderous "whump" ensued. A belch of flame shot out over the compound but, to Jos' disappointment, it seemed that only about half of the small fuel filled vials that were supposed to act like little Molotov cocktails had caught on fire. Nonetheless, as those landed, extensive fires started in the fuel they'd spilled.

A drifting spark fell into the still open compartment full of charged superconductors on one of the APCs. Yasso saw the flash of flame beside him as the fuel in the compartment caught, but then the insulating plastic, already weakened by the solvent action of the fuel, broke down. In a microsecond this released a sudden coruscating hellfire of electrical discharge, powerful enough to run a small city for several hours. It melted down half of the APC and flash cooked the luckless guard.

Steb reached the fence. Gasping for breath he looked for the hole he'd cut earlier.

Gripping the chain link he shook it in panic. Where was the damn hole? The skin on his back began to crawl as he imagined a kalsaw sighting in on him. He bolted to the right. Still no sign of the hole! He looked at the top of the fence with thoughts of trying to climb, but then he heard Jos' shout to his left. He ran to the hole and dove through while Jos held it open.

"Where the hell's Nigel?!"
"Dead..."
"Ohhh..."

\*\*\*

As the two remaining young men trudged home through the night, the enormity of the events just past struck home.

After the Stossa invasion, Nigel, Steb, and Jos, like everyone else, had waited for the Macos to swing into action. The Macos were the almost legendary elite of elite warriors. Formed by General Minguez in a war fifteen years earlier, the Macos had, by dint of special tactics and high tech weaponry, hamstrung their opponents. Cutting lines of supply and taking out leaders far behind enemy lines, the Macos had brought their adversary to a frustrated halt. Actually, Steb had been named Steban after an uncle who was the most highly decorated Maco of that war. His uncle had been killed in the last days of the war, but his medals hung proudly over Steb's family fireplace. An uncle Steb had never known, but whom he worshipped like so many people.

After this new invasion, everyone whispered eagerly of the time when the Macos would swing back into action. But, when they did, they were ineffectual and disorganized. It seemed that the wait had been in vain. Months and then years went by with no more than a few bitter failures and reactionary "roundups" of the resistance by the Stossa. Furtive conversations Steb picked up from the adults implied that the remaining Macos were old, tired, and, without General Minguez, leaderless.

The three buddies began with small acts of vandalism.

Soon they began scratching the fin of a shark in the paint of a Stossa vehicle after puncturing its tires. They began calling *themselves* "Macos".

Nigel had generally been their leader, though Steb credited himself with their best ideas. The truck, chocked with a bag of ice, on the hill above one of the Stossa "not so secret" police offices had been one of his best.

It was a Stossa truck, parked half a block up the street that made a "T" into the street right in front of a Stossa office. The one that they ran their not-so-secret police from. The truck was in front of a store that the "Macos" walked past on their way home from school almost every day. On this particular day, Steb had noticed that no one was parked below the truck.

Nigel had gotten into the truck and straightened out the wheels while Steb was buying a bag of ice a couple of blocks away.

Jos had been their lookout, although this was only after he'd repeatedly told them they were out of their minds.

With the back curb wheel chocked with a half empty bag of ice Nigel had let off the brake and taken the truck out of gear. The three boys had walked down and around the corner. The wait was interminable. Just as Steb finally resolved to walk back and check to see that something else wasn't blocking the wheel the truck shuddered! Then it broke loose and began to roll.

Steb tried to gape stupidly like the other onlookers. Someone on the other side of the street ran out as if to stop it, then saw where the truck was going and slowed to watch. A crowd of people watched it gather speed, roll swiftly across the intersection, jump the curb and plunge through the big plate glass window into the Stossa police office. It took out a column and the roof collapsed in that section. A few minutes later flames began to lick out around the truck.

The huge crowd of gawkers that gathered hindered the arrival of fire trucks. The crowd continued to impede the halfhearted efforts of the firemen while the structure itself burned completely to the ground.

Steb was bursting with enthusiasm when he got home. Yotel, his uncle on his mother's side, was there drinking beer with Steb's father, Lante. Yotel was drunk on his ass as usual and Lante was trying to keep him from finishing his latest beer. They'd already heard of the events at the police building and were heatedly discussing them.

Yotel taunted, "Almost like old Steban was back in town, eh Laaante?"

"Sure Yotel," Lante said disgustedly, "Steban would have known how a little fire down at the secret police building would run the Stossa *right out* of this country."

"Well it's a hell of a lot better than sitting around on our asses doing nothing! *Steban* would have been out doing *something* about those bastards!"

"Sober up Yotel!" Lante said disgustedly, "You—laying around drunk—you're providing almost as much resistance as the dear *departed* Steban."

Steb couldn't listen to this anymore. "Come on Dad. Are you trying to say that uncle *Steban* couldn't have done anything about the Stossa invasion?"

"Well kid, I guess I knew your uncle better than anyone else did." Lante glared at Yotel, "I never saw Steban bash his head on walls and I don't think he'd be setting fires down at the Stossa police station either."

"*I* think he would!"

"You tell him kid," slurred uncle Yotel.

Encouraged, Steb blurted out, "Yeah, and *I'm* carrying on in his tradition. Nigel, Jos and *I* are the ones who ran that truck into the Police station."

Lante's brown eyes flashed wide. Even his balding pate turned red with fury. He leapt to his feet, grabbed the front of Steb's shirt and pulled him close. He leaned his squat body over his son's slender one. "Are you *crazy*? You stupid little *shit*! You could've been *killed*! You have not even the *slightest* goddamn idea what you're doing or how dangerous it is! Do you think three *kids* could take on an entire country? You'd better not ever, *ever*, even *consider* doing that kind of crap again."

While the old man ranted on, Yotel stumbled out the back door without a word of support. Steb could neither think of a valid retort, nor work it in edgewise.

\*\*\*

105

At first taken aback and apologetic, Steb had slowly angered. After a few more meetings with Nigel and Jos, he'd begrudgingly admitted, if only to himself, that his father was a rank coward. Steb had always been embarrassed that the old fart was so out of shape, but Lante almost seemed proud of it, patting and rubbing his paunch for all the world to see. He couldn't even get a better job than warehouseman at the docks.

*Too chickenshit to apply for a better one no doubt.*

Lante never wanted to talk about his famous brother and Steb had always attributed it to the fact that Lante was the only member of his family to survive the earlier war. Now he realized the old man was *jealous* of Steban. Steb had never seen his father in this light before.

Recognizing his father's utter cowardice broke his heart.

\*\*\*

Despite Lante's warning, the Macos had persisted in their vandalism, judging their success by the security measures that the Stossa were forced to undertake. Now Stossa vehicles were almost always guarded or kept in a compound. The three "Macos" took pride in the fact that the Stossa were forced to use valuable military manpower round the clock just to keep some kids from vandalizing their equipment.

When the Stossa pulled in people from the neighborhood for questioning about "the sharks" the Macos became grateful that Lante's furious reaction had kept them from bragging about their exploits. They also started branching out to other areas of the city in order to diffuse the search.

Steb, fearing that his two friends recognized his father's cowardice, became the most reckless of the three. Even though he felt terrified inside, he projected bravado to hide his family's terrible secret. Though Jos protested repeatedly of the danger, Nigel spurred them ever onward and always found Steb willing to take one more risk.

In any case, Steb had always pictured them dying, if at all, in glory and as a group.

Now Nigel alone was dead...

No one knew how he'd died, except Steb and Jos.

How would they tell Nigel's mother?

\*\*\*

It was four in the morning when Jos and Steb split up at the edge of their own neighborhood—still unresolved about whether, or how, to tell Nigel's mom. To Steb's great relief Jos had never said the dreaded words, "I told you so."

Steb turned the corner into his alley. Damn! Every light in his house must be on! What was going on?

He crept from yard to yard and slowly up to his own front window. He saw his sister Lisa sprawled on the floor, her face bloody.

My God, dead?

No, she was breathing! Knocked out, with a bloody nose from the looks of it, but she moved a little.

Suddenly a Stossa soldier moved into view. The soldier's back was to Steb. He gestured at the couch with his kalsaw. Steb's mother sat on the couch, weeping and also bleeding. Fury raged up in Steb and he stepped over to launch himself through the door. Having no other weapon, he pulled out his triflanged awl.

Two iron arms clapped around him! One over his arms and one over his mouth! Lante's voice whispered sorrowfully in his ear, "Looks like they caught you this time, eh kid?"

Steb tried to wrench himself loose, but the old man kept him in a steel hard grip. How could the pudgy old geezer be so strong? Where was that soft paunch the old man was always patting and shaking his head over? As he dragged his son toward the garage Lante said, "They had poor Nigel's body with them when they first got here. They were pretty pissed; sounds like you really screwed up their truck compound."

At first, mortified over the disaster he had wrought upon his own family, Steb suddenly realized his father had just watched them beating his mother and sister without doing a goddamn thing! What's worse he wasn't *planning* to do a goddamn thing *and* didn't intend to let Steb do anything either! Rage flashed through him and he ripped his left arm loose and drove his elbow into the old man's gut. His arm rebounded off a rock hard abdomen and back into Lante's grip; a grip now *painfully* tight!

Lante shouldered the door to the garage open and dragged Steb inside without much apparent effort.

"OK kid, I'm gonna turn you loose, but you've gotta promise not to act like an asshole again, huh?"

After a moment, Steb nodded sullenly. His father's grip loosened, but slowly, ready to resume at the first false move. With disdain dripping from his words Steb said, "How *could* you just stand there and watch them beating Mom and Lisa? Are you completely spineless?"

Through clenched teeth fury his father said, "I stood and watched because it was the only way I could think to save *your* ass, you worthless little shit! God dammit! I told you to cut that sabotage shit out!

*You* are the proximate cause of what they've gone through! And you have the *balls* to sneer at me?! At least *I* can figure out they aren't going to seriously hurt Mom and Lisa until they know where you and I are."

"*Someone* has to stand up to those assholes!"

"Yeah, well," Lante said disgustedly, "that someone needs to be old enough and smart enough to wipe his own ass, kid... Now, do you think that we might be able to work *together* long enough to get your mother and Lisa out of there? Diving through a door into a room full of soldiers with armed kalsaws was only going to get you dead."

"There was only one!"

"Shit kid, *look* before you leap, at least around the corner!"

Embarrassed, hot tears coursed down Steb's cheeks. He sniffed, "What's *your* great idea then?"

The old man seemed to slump back, "You ever *used* a kalsaw, kid?"

"Hell no! They're useless to us; they won't fire at a Stossa in uniform. And the bastards *never* take their damned helmets off."

"Not true kid, especially of these kalsaws here." The older man pulled out a false panel concealed by the pegboard his tools hung on. There, gleaming greasily in the faint light from the house, were two kalsaws.

Steb was stunned! *How long have those damned things been there?* he wondered.

His dad took the two kalsaws down, wiping the oil off them with a rag. He pulled out extra magazines for each one and closed the panel. He held a kalsaw up into the dim light of the window. "Three tubes, kid. The middle one is the sight; really a fancy visual/infrared camera that takes in the view for a 20 degree arc around your point of aim, looking for heat or motion. It also looks for a digital infrared message to tell it 'friend or foe;' that's what the Stossa helmets and harnesses do. Not their uniforms. But, it has to be programmed with a new 'friend' message daily. These two haven't been programmed in years, so they'll shoot Stossa too. Upper tube is the laser; lower tube is an electric rail gun for the kinetic slugs. The laser delivers enough energy in each pulse to boil a liter of water and people are mostly water. 'Cause they're so small you've got seventy kinetic slugs. They have a velocity of 1500 meters per second and shatter on impact. They'll rip a human body in half."

"Cut the damn sermon… just show me the trigger and let's go."

There was a pause, "Kid, it's called a 'smart weapon' 'cause you *shouldn't let morons use 'em.* You've *got* to understand a weapon like this… hell if you don't, you're just as likely to rip your own mother to shreds."

Another pause. Lante eyed his son balefully. Steb finally nodded.

Lante went on, "Index trigger, laser. Middle finger, kinetic. That much is pretty simple. Feel this lever on your thumb?"

"Yeah."

"Down is safe. First click up and it fires at any hot images on the infrared, whenever the trigger is pulled. The laser will fire a burst of three, one at the left edge, one in the center, and one at the right edge. It'll fire at *any* hot object in its 20 degree cone. At the speed of light it *will* hit the object."

"The rail gun can turn its projectiles about 5 degrees from center bead and will do so in an attempt to strike the target, it is, however, possible to miss with the rail gun. When firing in this mode, wave the gun past the target and let it pick its shot. The kalsaw's 'puter will compensate for motion of the kalsaw and the motion of the object and it'll hit the object *almost every time.*"

"Click up a second time and it fires at any *moving* object. You don't usually want to do that, so the detent's weak there; makes it hard to screw up and set it on 'motion.'

"Third click up and it fires on manual every time you pull the trigger, right down the center bead; no auto aiming. It fires a burst of three if your thumb's still on the lever. If you take your thumb off of the lever, it fires single shots."

"A fourth click up and it fires on full automatic. Real waste of ammo and energy ... the kalsaw'll melt down after 30 seconds full auto. That's why it's so hard to make the final click."

Steb shook his head in amazement. *Where had the old man learned all this stuff?* "So *do* you have a plan, Dad?"

"Yeah. Here's the deal. You get in the car. As soon as I hear the starter, I break the window and take the bastards out with the kalsaw. You pull around front and we'll load the girls. If I get in trouble, you're my backup."

"What the hell? You put the kalsaw on auto and it'll take out Mom and Lisa!"

"I'll fire on manual."

"And take out a whole roomful of experienced soldiers, each with his kalsaw *on* auto. You've gotta be kidding! We go in together."

"*You* firing on manual is *not* going to improve the odds."

"I'll stand off to the side where my kalsaw can't 'see' Mom or Lisa and *I'll* use auto."

A long pause, "Not a bad idea, kid."

"I'm not a kid anymore... And I'm *not* an idiot!"

"You're right, kii... You're right, Steb. OK I'll take out the interrogator on manual, laser *and* kinetic. When the window breaks you wave down the rest of them on auto laser."

Suddenly the light coming in the window increased. The back porch light had come on. Through the window they could see three soldiers come out the door and down the stairs. Damn, they were coming out to search the garage! Steb flipped his kalsaw off safe.

When his father heard the kalsaw charging, he grabbed it out of Steb's hands and shut it off. "They'd hear that right away. And, if you'd fired it, they'd hear it in the house."

"What the hell *are* we going to do?" Steb whispered fiercely.

"There, hide behind the end of the bench."

"They'll see me!"

"Of course they will. When they do, stand up with your hands in the air and look scared. It'll keep them from noticing me."

Steb's father disappeared into the darkness and Steb crouched behind the bench, unable to believe that his father was so much of a coward that he would use his son as a distraction so *he* could hide. After what Lante'd allowed to happen to his own wife and daughter, Steb supposed it shouldn't be a surprise.

Steb didn't want to hide… but maybe he owed it to his family to try to save them by giving himself up. He crouched behind the end of the bench.

The door banged open and the lights came on. The first two soldiers came in talking to one another. They were having some kind of an argument in Stossa. They stopped just inside the doorway and now Steb saw his father's heavyset form, standing in the shadow behind the door. Lante's dark clothing and the clutter of tools had obscured him at first, but he wasn't really hidden at all. Without even looking around, the two soldiers walked into the middle of the small room, still arguing vehemently. One's kalsaw was still slung, but the other soldier's kalsaw was gripped in his arm and the high pitched whine emanating from it indicated it was already charged! The third soldier stopped and leaned back in the door frame, gazing up into the sky. They stopped arguing and glanced cursorily around the room. Steb thought with amazement, "They're going to miss me completely!" They turned on their heels to go back out.

They stopped abruptly. Why? Then Steb saw the kalsaw coming up to bear on his father.

The guard's eyes opened wide in amazement as his peripheral vision registered the shadowy figure behind the door. It was the fat old man, father of the kid they'd been looking for! How long had the chickenshit bastard been hiding out here while they beat up his wife and daughter? Well, it looked like he was going to get what was coming to him after all. Ala brought his kalsaw to bear with a sneer on his face and stopped Sotan with one hand. "Eh, Sotan, Wanob, what have we here?" He could see the old man turning to jelly before his eyes. The fat bastard dropped to his knees, hands raised in supplication, tears running down his quivering cheeks, the stench of urine filling the room from the large stain at his crotch. Wanob stepped around the door to look at the pitiful slob. The miserable bastard now had his face on the floor and was sobbing piteously. "Get up you worthless sack of shit!" Ala began to dread having to carry the fat bastard into the house—the ones who got this hysterical could rarely walk—Ala really preferred the sullen ones.

Steb looked on in shock. For a little while, when Lante'd dragged him out here, he'd begun to think that the old man had developed some backbone. Then he'd asked Steb to give himself up to

113

help Lante hide. Now to see his father crumple like this filled Steb with disgust.

*Shit!* Steb couldn't use the kalsaw; it'd kill Lante too. He picked up a half meter piece of two centimeter steel pipe that was lying on the lower shelf of the bench. He rose from his crouch and stepped toward the group at the door. At least the guards were all focused on his groveling father. One kicked Lante in the side, knocking him over. He began shouting at "the old fart" to get to his feet. The old man fell against the door, slamming it shut and knocking over a stack of concrete rebar that had been behind the door. Lante pulled a leg up under himself and promptly stumbled in the rebar scattering it all over the floor. Suddenly Steb saw his father's eyes flick to look at Steb's feet. Steb hefted the pipe, wondering where to strike? The helmet was good protection. He swung mightily at bottom of the guard's ear where it protruded beneath the helmet.

He thought distantly that the feel of the impact was similar to striking a watermelon. The guard dropped convulsing to the floor. Steb jerked the bloody pipe back to strike at the next guard, but that one was already twisting, falling, convulsively grasping. At a piece of rebar that protruded from beneath his breastbone!

*Oh my God!* Steb thought. So was the third guard as well! Steb realized that the flash of motion in his peripheral vision when Steb struck the first guard, had been his father exploding off the floor with a chunk of rebar in each hand. The rebar Lante had just plunged up under the guards' ribcages! Steb had always wondered why the rebar in the garage was cut off to points at 45 degree angles.

Now he knew.

Lante efficiently knocked the guards' helmets off so that, even while dying, they couldn't call on their radios. Even before they'd finished their death throes his father was working on their harnesses.

"Wearing the guards' harnesses and helmets will keep kalsaws from firing on us, at least if they're in the smart mode," Lante said, attaching a wire across the back of the harness and using a bolt cutter to cut through a heavy steel cable embedded in the harness.

"Why don't you just unbuckle it?"

"Deprograms the recognition codes." Lante grinned up at Steb, "Be a mess if your enemy could easily take the harnesses off of bodies in the field, eh?"

Lante picked up the helmets and showed Steb how to adjust their size and set the ear piece so they would hear Stossa communications.

They picked up their own kalsaws and headed out the door. There was a sudden query on the helmet net and Steb realized that listening in was practically worthless since he only spoke a few words of Stossa. To his shock he heard the voice of the first guard answering the query. He whirled to his father and realized that it had been his father imitating the nasal voice of the guard. *When the hell did the old man learn to speak Stossa?!*

With an even sicker feeling, he wondered if his father could be a secret collaborator.

Lante motioned Steb to crawl under the living room window to the other side. He rose up and saw that his father had been right, there were four more soldiers on the other side of the room. Shit! One of them had Lisa's blouse! Then she stepped into view. One hand over her breasts, other hand outstretched, Lisa was apparently asking for the blouse back. Damn! He clicked the kalsaw from infrared to manual, but he couldn't possibly take out five of them on manual before they killed Lisa on auto. He looked at his father. The older man simply held up his hand in the universal gesture, "Wait."

The soldier with the blouse made an obscene intimation with his fingers. How the hell could his father wait?! What was happening to Steb's mother?!

The soldier pantomimed Lisa removing her skirt. Steb's head pounded with rage. She stood up straight and turned, walking resolutely away from the guards.

The window exploded into a billion small pieces of glass! Steb convulsively crushed both triggers and swept the kalsaw over the group of guards. Goddamn, it only fired once, was it empty? It didn't hit even one of the guards!

Shit! The damn thing was still on manual! The guards were swinging their kalsaws toward the window and Steb as he flipped the lever back. He pulled the trigger again. Nothing happened! It must be empty! The guards were firing out the window now, he was dead! No, their kalsaws had fired into the warm house next door, missing Steb because of his Stossa helmet and harness. In a second *they* would go to manual, he started to jerk back from the window when his father's shouts finally penetrated his brain.

".... on safe dammit!"

Yes! He'd pulled the lever back too far! He flipped it forward and waved it over the soldiers with both the triggers down. Red laser flashes and the blue coruscation of the rail gun rewarded him.

The soldiers in the room practically exploded.

Steb stood, gaping at the destruction. Suddenly Lante was there, forcing the kalsaw's barrel up in the air. "Get the car!"

Steb broke from his reverie and sprinted for the garage. In two minutes he pulled around to the front street. Shit! Lante stood weaponless in front of the two women. He had a kalsaw jammed into his

116

back. It wouldn't see the signal from his helmet and harness there! That last soldier must have been somewhere else inside the house. Steb pulled up into the neighbor's driveway, opened the window and picked up the kalsaw that had been laying on the seat next to him. This time he checked carefully to be sure it was on manual. He looked carefully into the sight and centered on the guard's head. *Damn! What if the soldier convulses and shoots Lante in the back?* Steb increased the magnification and swung down to the guard's hand where he centered in on the man's trigger finger. Carefully he squeezed the laser trigger. A flash on the screen and the guard was dancing back, the kalsaw falling from his destroyed hand. Lante whirled and dropped the guard with a *kick to the head!*

*How the hell had the old man gotten his foot* that *high?!*

A moment later, Lante was hustling the women out the door. Suddenly Steb's mother whirled and went back in. She returned a moment later with something in her hand.

As they drove away, Lante spluttered at his wife. "What the *hell* was *so* important you risked our lives to go back in there for it?"

"If you're going to organize the resistance, you're going to need your medals. The people will rally to them."

"They aren't 'his medals' mom." Steb ground out as he slammed the car out onto the street. "The people aren't going to 'rally' to Steban's milquetoast brother."

His mother said, a sad tone in her voice, "Son, Steban didn't *have* a brother. When the rest of his family was killed at the end of the war, he changed his name to Lante because he didn't want people thinking of him as a killer."

Steb turned wide eyed to stare at his father, goosebumps running over his body.

Lante stared back calmly. Finally he said, "I guess I can't stop you trying to revive the Macos, kii… son. So," he paused, then continued heavily, "I suppose I'd better start helping you. Otherwise you're *surely* gonna get yourself killed." His voice took on a wistful tone, "I'd never forgive myself if that happened."

Steb drove on in dazed silence for a minute, *My hero… is my father?* he thought, almost plaintively. Finally, he turned toward Jos' house.

Jos probably needed some help.

### The End

Inspired (distantly) by the movie Target

# PORTER

Allie Dans formed her first "port" shortly after she turned eleven.

She was at her cousin Mindy's birthday party. It was a hot summer day and Aunt Stella hotfooted it across the burning pool deck to hand Allie and Mindy each a glass of icy Kool-Aid. In the humidity, the glass was sweating nearly as much as Allie was. She bowed her strawberry blonde head over it in puzzlement. "Aunt Stella, how does the water get to the outside of the glass?"

Stella looked where Allie was focused and then, in an uncertain tone her aunt posited, "Maybe the heat makes the glass leaky."

"For God's sake, Stella!" Allie's dad said without opening his eyes behind his sunglasses. "It's condensation! The cold condenses water onto the glass!" He laid his head back against the deck recliner and adjusted the brim of his hat to cover his eyes again.

Not knowing what "condensation" was, Allie thought to herself that her dad's explanation wasn't at all helpful. Big words, but a complete lack of enlightenment. However, she didn't want to ask her dad about it. He'd subject her to a long and complicated explanation. Everybody thought her Dad was a genius, but he had a tendency to explain things in such detail that they became even more confusing than they were to begin with.

Still thinking about it, she squinted and pictured a tiny tunnel through the glass, from the Kool-Aid on the inside, to the air on the outer surface. As she visualized it, to her astonishment a big drop welled up on the surface of the glass, right where she was imagining the hole! During her moment of startlement, the drop stopped growing, but, when she

119

concentrated on it again, it then resumed growing and began dribbling. Eventually it became a steady stream. After a moment, the level of Kool-Aid in the glass fell to the level of Allie's "hole" and the stream slowed down and stopped. Allie picked up the glass and tasted the dribble. Yep, Kool-Aid. She tasted the other tiny drops covering the rest of the glass… they were just water.

Allie took a sip and looked over at Mindy. Mindy was raising her glass to her lips. Allie focused on Mindy's glass and was rewarded with a dribble down Mindy's chin. "Ew!" The fastidious Mindy set the glass down and wiped her chin, staring suspiciously at the rim of the glass and running her finger over it. She wiped sticky fingers on the table top with distaste. Then Mindy brightened, "Let's get in the pool!"

The next night, when the Dans family sat down to dinner, Allie looked at the condensation on the surface of the glass of iced tea her mom had just served. Remembering, she held the glass up over her plate and pictured a tunnel through the bottom of the glass; sure enough the bottom of the glass began to drip onto her plate when she formed the port.

She looked over at her dad. He'd brought a paper to the dinner table and was studying it. His reading at the dinner table always made Mom mad, but he did it a lot anyway. He lifted his glass. Allie made a port just behind the lip and giggled as she saw tea run down his chin. "What the hell?!" he swore, setting the glass down and reaching for a napkin. He looked suspiciously over at Allie who was desperately trying to stifle a giggle. Then he examined the glass. It was one of their regular glasses. It didn't have a convoluted surface like dribble glasses have. In fact, it had a perfectly smooth, one could say "glassy," surface. "What the hell?!" he repeated and looked at Allie again. "Did you do that somehow?"

Hand over her mouth, Allie giggled a little more while nodding her head.

He looked back at the glass, running a finger over its surface below the rim, both inside and outside.

Puzzled, he asked, "How?"

"I just made a leak like Aunt Stella said."

"What?"

"Well, she said 'the heat makes the glass leaky.' *You* said it was 'condensation.' *I* made a little tunnel through the glass 'cause I don't know how to make it 'leaky'."

"What?!"

"She said 'the heat made-'"

"I *know* what she said! It was stupid! Heat *doesn't* make glass leaky!"

Allie bowed her head, "Sorry." Her dad was mostly pretty nice, but when he got mad, he could be scary.

"No, *how* did *you* make the glass leak?"

In a small voice, "I made a little tunnel..."

"There isn't a tunnel there!"

A smaller voice, "*Only* when I think it."

Goosebumps raised the hair on Albert Dans' neck.

"What?" he said turning to stare at his daughter.

Allie whispered, "Only when I think it."

He was holding the glass in the air looking at it. To his astonishment, a small stream of tea appeared just below the glass and splattered onto his plate. It wasn't coming from the glass, or through the glass, it was appearing in space about an inch below the bottom of the glass then streaming straight down! He dropped the glass, leaping to his feet and knocking his chair over backwards, "Holy shit!" The glass shattered on his dinner plate, breaking the plate as well.

With a small cry Allie ducked her head and bolted from the table, running up the stairs to her room.

Allie's mom looked away from Stephen, Allie's towheaded 4-year old brother. "What just happened?!"

Al set the chair back up, shook his head and said, "*I* have *no* idea." He got a broom and mop, cleaned up the mess, then dished himself another plate. He took his plate and Allie's up to her room.

Allie had curled up on the bed and when he entered, she looked apprehensively up through her hair at her dad.

Speaking as calmly as he could, Al said "You're not in trouble; I brought you your dinner." Al sat down on the corner of her bed, putting her plate on her desk.

Allie pulled her hair partly back off her face to peer more clearly at her dad, who in fact *didn't* seem angry. "I'm not hungry."

"OK." Her dad calmly began eating his own dinner. "Do you think you could show me what you can do with your 'tunnels' later?"

"OK." Allie got off the bed, wiped her nose and went over to sit at her desk. She picked at her food for a while, but didn't eat much.

"Are you done?" Her dad asked, nodding at her plate.

"Yes." She said in a small voice.

He picked up both of their plates and took them down to put in the dishwasher. Shortly, he appeared back in her door with two bowls of ice cream. She raised her eyebrows. "But I didn't eat all my dinner?"

"I know." He gave her a little grin, "*Some* rules have to be broken occasionally."

They ate their ice cream in silence. When it was gone Al asked, "Ready to make me a 'tunnel'?" Allie nodded, rubbing her wrist under her nose again. He heard a spraying sound and looked down in astonishment to see a tiny jet of water shooting into the bottom of his ice cream bowl. Though his initial reaction was to shout, he managed to restrain himself to an almost calm, "What the hell!?" He looked back up at Allie who was watching the spray too. He swallowed the storm of questions exploding in his brain to say simply, "Where is *that* tunnel coming from?"

"The pipe in the wall there." She pointed over his shoulder with her chin. The spray stopped.

"How did you know there was a pipe in the wall?"

"I sorta feel them... Don't you?"

Her dad made a choking sound, "No... I don't think anybody can... 'cept maybe you." He began asking a seemingly endless list of questions, most of which Allie couldn't answer. She dribbled water out of glasses and sprayed it out of pipes. After a while she developed a headache and became unable to create more than a tiny tunnel. Still he wanted her to do more.

Finally her mother came in and watched what was going on with growing astonishment. After a while though, she said, "Al, she needs to rest. It's past her bedtime."

He turned to snap at his wife, then looked back at Allie, all droopy around the edges. "OK, Sarah." He turned back to his daughter, "Allie, we'll go into my lab tomorrow and learn more about what you can do, okay?"

Allie sighed and put on her pajamas. She wasn't looking forward to it. Tomorrow she and Mindy had been going to hang out at the pool. Her head was throbbing. Her mom got her a Tylenol and she curled up to sleep with her cat, Oscar.

Her dad spent hours on the internet trying to find credible evidence of teleportation or whatever the hell this phenomenon was. Not even a "less than credible" claim of the same phenomenon was to be found.

The next morning Allie's dad got her up early to take her in to his lab in the physics department at the University. He ignored her protests about going swimming with Mindy. When her mother said something about it, he just told her to let Aunt Stella know that Allie was "busy." At the lab, they did measurements until Allie's head was splitting again. Her eyes would hardly stay open. They rested over lunch at Burger King, then started again.

Dr. Dans' magnetic and electrical field measurements around Allie showed nothing different from those about his own head. Measurements around the ports found oddly "swirling" fields. Samples of distilled water and some organic solvents that had been through ports were put aside for assay by a friend in the chemistry department. Later Al learned that there were no detectable changes from the control specimens that hadn't been "ported." Bacteria and yeast that had been ported continued to live.

When Allie got too tired to make ports again, her dad spent time on the phone with a friend at the medical school trying to arrange an MRI of her head, "To see if there were any unusual structures."

Other than the friend at the medical school whom her dad only told that she had "an unusual ability," no one else was told that Allie was the center of a new research program.

When the MRI was finished no one could find any recognizable difference between her brain and the brains of ordinary people.

Dr. Dans' grad student kept working on Dans' grant funded research project, getting barked at when he interrupted the "Allie research" with questions about their funded study. Everyone that came into the lab was told that Allie was there to "keep her out of her Mom's hair" or to "learn how science worked." Her dad strictly forbade her to tell any of her friends about her new ability or to do any tricks for *anyone* except him. Videos he made of the effect in action carefully excluded Allie from the field of view.

Needing her cooperation, Al was very pleasant to her, ordering out lunch from all her favorite restaurants and setting up a computer for her to use between testing episodes. But, she was there in the lab all day almost every day! Even most weekends!

The rest of Allie's summer was ruined with 12-hour days at the lab. She soon began to look forward to the start of school; simply because it would provide a break from her dad. Her mother and father had started to argue about it; out of her presence, but she could hear them fighting through the walls.

At the end of her first day back at school Allie was dismayed to see her dad's car parked in front of the school. She opened the door, "Dad! I've got homework!"

Distractedly he looked up from the paper he'd been reading and smiled at her, "I know, Kiddo. It'll just be for an hour. Besides you can do your homework during my setup time between the first and second experiments." He blinked, "Your new clothes look really nice!"

Sullenly, Allie got in the car. As she expected, one hour turned into two. An angry call from her mother was needed to get them home for dinner.

Her dad became more and more frustrated as test after test demonstrated odd, but miniscule physical phenomena around the port area at both entrance and exit. There was a tiny rotating electrical field, fluctuating magnetic phenomena and a slight attractive force, possibly gravitational, around the "ports." The electromagnetic and possible gravitational fields were so tiny they were at the limits of detection for the most sensitive measuring devices he had available. Worse, the measurements would be different from one repetition of a port setup to the next! He worried that *all* he had detected was the "noise" in the measurements.

Dans determined that materials only flowed through the ports like they would through a hose, from high pressure to low pressure. Interestingly, Allie was able to open ports over a longer distance when the flow of material through the port was energetic. Thus a port from a high pressure pipe could be opened over a much greater distance than a port from a glass of water. When it was opened over a long distance, the water sprayed out with little pressure, as if the energy of that pressure was being used to cross the distance. When Allie was fresh, she could open a port as big as 3mm in diameter, but the diameter dropped off quickly as she got tired.

Her dad had no handle on the phenomenon, and therefore could not reproduce it; much less magnify the effect as he'd hoped. He became more and more irritated and, though it seemed impossible, even more absent-minded. Allie's parents started to fight. Her mother threatened divorce if he didn't let Allie have time to "be a kid."

He finally agreed to no more than ten hours of testing per week.

Then, Thanksgiving weekend came and Allie got sick. High fevers and a cough, the doctor diagnosed "that flu that's going around" and prescribed "rest and fluids." He said, "Don't worry, it'll get better."

While she was sick, Allie discovered that she couldn't make a port. To her dad's great dismay, when the flu resolved, she didn't recover the ability. He checked her morning and evening, first in dismay, then in frustration, then in anger, accusing her of simply *refusing* to make ports.

But, as the weeks and then months passed, it seemed that the startling physical phenomenon/ability was likely gone forever.

Allie hadn't liked her dad's constant queries about her ability. They'd rapidly gone from exciting, to irritating, to maddening.

She'd begun to dislike *him*.

*Then* she started puberty.

Allie was a sullen teenager. Sullen and angry about everything, and *especially* about her lost ability. She locked herself in her room for hours on end, playing electric guitar into headphones. Sarah offered to pay for lessons. Allie didn't want them, preferring to teach herself by watching YouTube videos.

Years passed.

Her parents had no idea just how good Allie had become on the guitar because they couldn't hear the sound in her headphones, and she balefully refused to let them listen. If they insisted, she hooked up her amp and thrashed loud distorted pieces with dissonant chords.

They learned not to ask.

Dr. Dans spent long hours going over and over the data that he'd accumulated, trying to find *something* that he had missed that could explain the phenomenon. He spent endless hours searching the literature and the Internet for someone else who may have made similar observations. He felt certain that there must be some physical way to reproduce what his daughter had been able to do for those few fleeting months, though sometimes he wondered if he'd imagined it. When Sarah questioned him, he admitted that there seemed to be little practical use for a port no bigger than 3mm over distances of no more than 20-30 feet, but, if the phenomenon could just be understood, he hoped it could be scaled up.

Allie's mother gradually forgave her husband for his earlier behavior, but when he occasionally stopped by Allie's room to ask her to "try to create a port" again, he could count on Sarah being there to tell him to "stop badgering the girl."
"Surely," she'd say, "Allie will let you know if she starts to be able to do it again."

Allie's teenage years passed slowly and morosely. Though she never seemed to study, her parents couldn't complain because she got excellent grades. She joined a band and spent long hours at practice with them. They played a few gigs, but parents were never invited, either to practices, or to their very occasional gigs. In fact, they were actively discouraged from attending.
Then, in her senior year of high school, her mother knocked on Allie's constantly closed bedroom door, first lightly, then loudly. Finally she pounded on it. Sarah heard her daughter's angry voice, "Come in." Wondering how to fix the yawning chasm between her and her daughter, Sarah opened the door. Guitar on her lap, Allie sat on the floor in baggy jeans, and a ripped t-shirt. She'd apparently cut her hair to a ragged inch long and dyed it black since her mother saw her going out the door that morning. As usual her room was a disaster, clothes strewn everywhere. Gritting her teeth, Sarah ignored the mess. She tried to sound chipper and upbeat, "Hey Allie, I'm hoping that we can plan a trip to visit some of the colleges you're interested in?"
"I'm not going to college."
Startled, "What?!?!"
Grimly, "Not going."

"Of *course* you're going, what did you *think* you were going to do?"

"Band's going on the road."

"You can't do that! We won't *allow* it."

"I'm eighteen, you can't tell me what to do anymore… Well you could make me move out *now,* I guess. Do you want me to?" Allie raised an eyebrow.

"What!? Where do you think you'd live?"

"Friends, or the homeless shelter." She shrugged, "I'd have to work it out, so I hope you'll give me a little warning if you're tossing me."

A tear formed and ran down her mother's cheek. "Never," she croaked. She turned suddenly and left.

"Close my damned door!" Allie shouted after her. Then after a minute, she got up and closed it herself. She wondered if "never" had referred to the homeless shelter, or to going on the road?

Months of shouting, pleading, arguments and long glowering silences passed without any change in Allie's resolution. She was a musician, she wasn't going to college. She might go to college if music didn't work out, but she was *sure* she was going to have a career in music. Her mother got little support in the battle from Allie's dad, who, as usual, seemed too distracted to get very involved in the argument.

The morning after Allie's high school graduation Sarah Dans knocked on her door to ask what she'd like for breakfast, but there was no answer. When she opened the door she was astonished to see that Allie's room had been straightened up. Not great, but better than it had been in years. Then, with a sinking heart she saw that the guitar and amp were gone. There was a note on the bed. "We've got gigs in Atlanta."

No "goodbye," no mention of when she'd be back, no mention of where in Atlanta.

Sarah Dans sank down on Allie's bed and had a good long cry. When she had herself in control she called Allie's cell phone, but it went straight to message. Sarah hung up and tried again. This time when it went to message, in a trembling voice Sarah said, "Sorry we didn't get to see you this morning. Wish you all the luck in the world." Her voice broke, "Call if you need anything."

Sarah cried for a while longer.

Several days passed before Albert Dans noticed that his daughter was missing. He asked Sarah about it and, when Sarah said that she was on the road, doing her music, he nodded distractedly and went back to the paper he was reading on wormhole theory. Sarah didn't think he'd actually comprehended the calamity that had befallen their little family.

In actual fact, Allie's dad had given up on understanding the port phenomenon for a couple of years, but then recently had awakened in the middle of the night with an idea regarding quantum tunneling and how very low-power electromagnetic fields, such as a brain *could* generate, *might* allow particles to appear at a new location. So his port research was back on, full speed ahead. He spent every waking moment thinking about it.

\*\*\*

The band was on break and Allie walked out behind the bar to hang out with her bandmates. She sat at the corner of a little deck looking up at the stars while the three guys shared a cigarette over by the door. She knew they smoked dope too, because she could smell it on their clothes, but they knew better than to smoke it around her. They bought what they used in each town and *never* kept a stash in their van.

Allie'd laid down the law. They didn't drink more than one beer during a set either. Joe arranged their gigs, ran their finances and was their nominal "leader," but Allie was by *far* their best musician. Her guitar licks and eerie vocals were what commanded the substantial fan following they'd developed so far. They *all* knew that the band would be just another bunch of "wannabes" without her. So, when she made a rule, they followed it.

The back door of the bar slammed open and a large, obviously drunk man stumbled out. "Where's Eva?" he slurred.

Eva was Allie's stage name, but she didn't like talking to drunks so she turned back to continue looking up into the sky.

"Where's Eva?!" the man said with some irritation. Out of the corner of her eye, Allie saw the big guy tap forcefully on Joe's shoulder. It looked like the guys had been trying to ignore the drunk too. Joe looked up at him.

"Where's Eva?!"

Joe shrugged and turned back to reach for the cig. The big guy shoved him and said ominously, "You know where she is!"

Allie sighed, then said, "I'm over here. Are you a fan?"

"Of you babe! Not the rest of these losers... only you." He waved a deprecating hand at the rest of the band as he lurched her way.

Allie wrinkled her nose, "We're a band, not a one person show."

The man came too close, invading her personal space. His breath stank of beer and garlic. "Hey, *I* can set you up wi' shum *real* musicians! *You* could really be on your way." He grasped her elbow.

She looked down at his hand. "Please let go of me."

"Aw, I'm jes' bein' friendly." His hand stayed put.

She looked up into his unfocused eyes. "Please, let, go!" The other band members were shuffling her way. Obviously, they wanted to help her get rid of this guy, but he was *huge*. Forcing him to let her go would be a pretty dangerous endeavor and they hadn't joined a band because they liked to fight. Joe turned and trotted back to the bar, presumably looking for a bouncer.

The big guy pulled on her arm, "Lesh go shumwhere an' talk." He peered at her. "Heeyy, you're really beautiful, ya' know?" His eyebrows went up as if she should be astonished at this revelation. "Why d' you wear such ugly clothes?"

Allie resisted the pull on her elbow, but it inexorably pulled her up off the bench she'd been on. She took a few reluctant steps with him. His grip on her arm *hurt*. Startled she realized that this guy could be a *real* problem. *Not* just an annoyance, but a real honest to god *problem*. She jerked and twisted on her arm, trying to break it loose. He was pulling her out toward the parking lot!

He said, "Heeyy, don' be sush a downer, we're jus' gonna go si' in my car and talk about your career." He seemed oblivious to the fact that Allie was pulling as hard as she possibly could to go the other way. Her feet were sliding on the pavement, and her struggles slowed him not at all. Allie's heightened senses were focused on the big man including the sense only she had. The one that allowed her to feel the pressure of the blood flowing through his arteries. Although her ability to make ports had actually returned the week after that Thanksgiving years ago, Allie had carefully kept the secret completely to herself. She certainly hadn't wanted her dad to know about it! Allie hadn't made a port in a couple years because they seemed useless except as "party tricks" and she was worried that such a "party trick" would somehow come to the attention of her dad or some other scientist who'd be all over her for more testing. She thought again of letting blood out of an artery in the big man in an effort to stop him. She had thought of this "weapon" aspect years ago, but "back of napkin" calculations had determined that she couldn't hold a port open long enough to even weaken a big man like this from blood loss. *Maybe if I make him think he has a bloody nose he'll let me go?*

Allie sensed the vessels in the man's head. There was a big one in his neck right next to his windpipe! He suddenly started to cough. At first it was just a little; then big wracking coughs doubled him over. Her bandmates were startled to see blood on the hand he'd used to cover his mouth. He let go of Allie's arm and she patted him on the back. "That's a bad sounding cough. Probably ought to go to the ER and have it checked out. Especially coughing up blood like that." Her tone fairly dripped with false concern.

A bouncer trotted up, Joe behind him. "What's going on?" he said with authority. Then he stepped back, looking a little apprehensively at the coughing man-mountain who'd just stood to his full height and taken a long gasping breath.

Allie smiled up at him. "I'm not sure, but this fellow has suddenly developed a terrible cough and he's bringing up blood. Can you help him get some medical attention? We've got to get back for another set." She grabbed Joe by the elbow and tugged, "Let's go guys." Shaking their heads the band started back into the bar, turning occasionally to look back at the big fellow who was bent over again, hands on his knees. The coughing had cut back to an occasional wet hack. Just as they went in the door he threw up a large quantity of foul smelling bloody beer.

The next day, Joe bought each of them a can of Mace. Allie's was a little pink cartridge to go on a keychain. She never carried a purse, but she started carrying the Mace in the front pocket of her trademark saggy jeans.

\*\*\*

Despairing of understanding the port phenomenon alone, Dans had recently decided to try collaboration. He'd spent months going over the data he had from the past in light of his quantum tunneling idea. Such tunneling over a distance, aided by fields, still seemed promising, but he hadn't been able to develop any hardware that would make it happen. He started wondering if a fresh viewpoint on his data would shake something loose.

The question soon became, not whether, but *who* to collaborate with.

The other academics in his department were too fusty to be interested. Besides, they were all specialized in their own small areas that seemed unlikely to be related to the porting phenomenon.

People from other universities would be too far away for the kind of intense collaboration that he envisioned. Academics also would want to see the phenomenon reproduced, a first principle in science, before they would be interested. However, Randall Forst, one of Dans' old graduate students, had established a thriving private enterprise right there in the city. As a grad student, he'd always been better at the engineering than the theory side of physics. He'd demonstrated a real talent for turning out excellent research equipment and was making a very good living doing just that. The man had a phenomenal talent for producing devices no one else had been able to concoct and had written a string of lucrative patents.

Albert made an appointment with Forst and then spent several entire evenings going over the literature that he had accumulated that might be relevant. He wanted everything fresh in his mind for this meeting.

\*\*\*

"Eve of Destruction" had become an east coast phenomenon. The crowds at their gigs had gotten so big that they were now being booked into small to medium concert halls instead of the bars they'd started out in. Joe had been interviewing "managers" and they'd moved from their van into a bus.
This morning they'd all gathered in a coffee shop to talk to one of the manager candidates. Allie came back from the restroom to find him at the table with the other band members. Immediately she thought that he didn't fit their image. He seemed much too slick. He wasn't wearing a suit, but looked like he was. When she sat down across from him he looked mildly startled. "Holy shit! Eva, you're gorgeous! Why don't you dress like this for your shows?"
Allie glanced down at herself. She was wearing a snug midriff t-shirt, cutoffs and sandals. "Doesn't fit our music."
Joe said, "Give it up Steve. Yes, she's beautiful, but she wants us to succeed on the music, not her sex appeal."
"*Come on*! It's hard enough to make it in this business. For God's sake, you've *gotta* play *every* card you're dealt!"
Allie got up from the table. "Joe, let me know when you've got someone else for us to talk to?"
They all watched wistfully as she walked out the door. The guy they'd been interviewing said, "Joe, you've got to talk some sense into her! Are you the leader of this band or what?"
"Yeah," he chuckled ruefully, "I'm the 'leader,' but I do exactly what she says, just like the rest of the guys."

\*\*\*

Dans and Forst had just watched a split screen video with two views at right angles of absolutely nothing but a black background. The start of the video showed the setup of the two cameras and the black background cards and the lights. The split screen views showed the black background for 20 seconds, then, suddenly a spray of water erupted in the middle of the space, shooting upward out of nothingness. For that video Allie had opened a port from a cold water pipe in the lab to the spot at the focal point of the cameras.

Forst's head jerked back, eyes wide. "What just happened?"

Dans looked at him intently, "Something like a wormhole was just opened from a vessel containing pressurized water to the viewing area. The vessel was about 15 feet from the visible opening you saw on the video." Dans didn't want to say it just came from a water pipe in the wall. Didn't sound sophisticated enough.

Forst raised an eyebrow, "This is real?"

"Absolutely."

"Because it'd be pretty easy to fake with a good video editing program…" He trailed off tentatively.

Grimly, Albert said, "That video has not been manipulated at all. Not even an adjustment of brightness or contrast." He ran the same segment, and then others, running them repeatedly to let Forst look for video editing artifacts.

Forst turned to Dans, "Wow! Amazing. Can you bring the equipment here? Or do I need to go to your lab to look at it? Will the University let you sell me the manufacturing rights?"

Albert looked down at the table. His jaw bunched and he muttered, "I can no longer reproduce the phenomenon."

"What?" Forst guffawed and slapped his knee. "'If you can't reproduce it, it ain't real.' I'm pretty sure I'm quoting *you* correctly on that one!"

"It was reproduced hundreds of times and I collected reams of data!" Dans said hotly, "I just can't reproduce it anymore…" He trailed off.

Forst leaned back in his chair, "You have *got* to be shitting me!"

"I'm looking for a collaborator that can go over the data I obtained, see what I've missed and help me figure out how to do it again. And to do it bigger and better."

Forst looked up at the ceiling. An irreproducible phenomenon would be worthless. On the other hand, if *he* could figure out what had gone wrong with the equipment, which *was* kind of his specialty, *and* they could scale it up - the possibilities seemed tremendous! They started to talk over rights, how they would share them and the University's inevitable piece of the pie since Dans was employed by them.

\*\*\*

Thunder rolled off Joe's fingertips as they drummed on the low string of his electric bass. A spotlight gradually illuminated him, dressed entirely in black, standing in the center of the stage, back slightly arched and legs spread a little more than shoulder width. The crowd, which had been gathering excitement during the agonizingly long bass note, started to whoop, holler and whistle. Shan kicked the bass drum once to produce a powerful thump that echoed back and forth across the packed medium sized arena. Another thump, then the crack of a snare lit a spot on the snare drum. That spot gradually enlarged to encompass the entire drum set as Shan established a simple, solid beat. Joe's rolling bass thunder developed punctuations to match the beat established on the drums and then a spot faded in on their big Leslie speaker. The rotor spun up and a Hammond organ chord filled gradually in over the beat as another spot came up on Davis at the keyboards. The crowd, frenzied now, began to chant, "E-va! E-va! E-va!"

The unmistakable evanescent sound of Allie's guitar faded slowly into the mix adding to the pulse of the sound, but still carrying that first chord. A chord which had now been sustained for so long that the listeners were anxiously waiting for a change. The pulse sped gradually and Allie and Davis added some higher notes to the chord, but the listeners' anxiety for a chord change simply built, and built, and built.

When Joe raised the long neck of his bass guitar and chopped down with it, the next chord finally blossomed, and another spot lit Allie. It was hard to tell how slender and tall she was in her trademark ripped baggy jeans and heavy vest festooned with charms. Spiky black hair stuck up out of a visor that shaded her face. The crowd went wild as she leaned to the mike from a wide stance,

"Another may be
The master of my fate
But *I* will be
The captain of my soul

Over deep seas
I'll sail this soul
Against the breeze
And through those shoals"

The crowd rocked slowly back and forth as if in a trance. Her eerie vocal blended perfectly with Davis's simple baritone harmony. Some ecstatic fans fainted and were carried out of the arena. Hundreds of others had been turned away from the sold out concert.

***

Forst was appalled. Dans had provided him with data out the wazoo, but claimed that the apparatus that had created the ports had been destroyed. When asked for the remnants of the destroyed apparatus, Dans said that it "had been completely demolished in one of the tests and had been put in the trash." Construction notes and diagrams? Didn't exist! It had been "an accidental side effect of a couple of unrelated pieces of equipment purchased for something else and misconnected."

Photographs of the effect were abundant. Pictures of the device creating the effect? Nonexistent! Forst wasn't just appalled, he was pissed. Dans was obviously hiding something about the apparatus. This could be huge! He was sure he could make another device and that *he* could make it work, but Dans wouldn't give him *any* idea how the first one had been constructed. Dans wanted them to "try to figure out another way to create the same fields."

What a crock of shit! If you'd built one working airplane, you wouldn't send an engineer into a closet to "build something that flies" with no more guidance than "it's been done before" would you? Forst felt a band tightening around his head and knew that his blood pressure was up again.

Dans was coming over and they were going to have a serious talk!

Al Dans knocked on Forst's office door, hoping that Forst had finally been able to produce some kind of prototype that could generate the funny twisting electric field effects that he'd measured around Allie's ports. Forst had been getting really uptight and demanding, though. Al had begun strongly thinking of looking for a different collaborator. Nonetheless, he was genuinely surprised to see the bright red fury on Forst's face when he stepped into the room. "What's the matter?" he began.

Forst exploded. "What's the matter? *What's* the matter! For Chrissakes! You've got me wasting hundreds of thousands of dollars on an important project with both of my hands tied behind my back! *That's* what's the matter! What's the matter is that you need to tell me how your *first* goddamned machine worked! I'm not spending another dime on this *piece of shit* project while you pretend you don't have any idea how the original device was constructed."

Dans rocked back in astonishment. Even when Forst had been a grad student, Al had seen the man get pretty irritated when devices didn't work as expected. But Dans had never seen this much rage before. And *never* directed at himself! He swallowed and shrugged, "Well, OK, let's just give up on it then." To himself, he thought, *I certainly don't want to continue working with someone who has such a temper. I guess I'll just have to find another collaborator.*

Forst's eyebrows shot up his crimson forehead. "Give up? Give up! *I'm* the one with hundreds of thousands invested! We are *not* giving up! *You* are going to tell me *how* the first *damned* model worked!"

Dans made placating motions with his hands, "Randy, I've told you, I don't *know* how it worked."

"That's a load of crap!" Forst hurled a vase off his desk and it exploded against the wall behind Dans. "You're going to tell me! And you're gonna to tell me *now*!"

Flinching in startlement from the vase, Dans turned quickly to the door. To his surprise he found the exit blocked by a large man with a goatee. Al turned back to Forst, "Let's talk about this some more when you've calmed down."

His face dark, Forst ground out, "I'm *not* going to calm down. YOU, on the other hand, are going to provide some answers *today*. NOT after I've calmed down. *Today*, dammit!"

\*\*\*

After signing autographs until their fingers ached, Eve of Destruction stumbled out to their tour bus. Allie turned on her phone and plugged it in. It immediately started chirping. She pulled off her shirt and peered blearily at the screen. It listed scores of calls and messages from her mother. There were almost always a few, but this was *way* more than usual. She virtually never listened to any of them, though recently the cold attitude she'd held toward her parents had started to melt.

Then Allie saw there was a text from her little brother Stephen. *That* was unusual. Her heart skipped a beat as she touched the icon. "Sis, pls call home. Dad missing for three days. Mom going crazy."

A chill ran down Allie's spine. She leaned her head back against the wall. *Missing!? Could he have run off with a girlfriend or something?* Somehow she knew that wasn't true. It just didn't fit with her dad's dreamy eyed focus on physics. *Damn! It's the middle of the night. I'll call in the morning and he'll probably be home by then. It'll save a lot of trouble.* She pulled off her jeans and crawled under the sheet, but then lay staring at the roof of the bus. Finally, with a sigh, she got up, hit the shower and started washing the black crap out of her hair. They didn't have another concert for four days and it was only a two hour drive home from here.

\*\*\*

The doorbell rang and Sarah Dans nearly dropped her coffee. Her heart thumped in her chest. Since Al had gone missing she feared every ring for the potential bad news it might bring. She took a deep breath and went to the door. *Is it the police? No, it's a young woman.* With despair, she thought, *Oh no, probably some chipper door to door sales girl!* Sarah had just decided to pretend she wasn't home, when the young woman simply opened the door and stepped inside!

Allie!

Sarah threw her arms around the daughter she hadn't seen for a year and a half, sobbing uncontrollably. "You got my messages!"

Allie hugged her mom, reluctant to say that she wouldn't have listened to the messages if it hadn't been for Stephen. On the other hand, she wondered, why not? What had this plump, pleasant, woman ever done to deserve the disdain Allie had held her in for the past eight or so years? She held her mom tighter, suddenly crying herself. "Have you heard anything?" Her mom leaned back, looking into Allie's eyes and shaking her head. Allie found her heart sinking. All the way home she'd been thinking that she'd get home, and her dad would have showed up, and *she'd* be pissed. Now, confronted with the reality that he was still gone, she found herself thinking wistfully of the good times they'd had as a family. All the things that had irritated her so… seemed so trivial now.

Allie and her mom went in and sat at the breakfast table. Sarah jumped back up, "Let me get you something to eat!"

"No! I'm fine. Sit. Tell me what happened."

Instead, Sarah went to the stairs and yelled up, "Steve, Allie's home! Come on down!" She returned to the table and just sat staring at her daughter for a moment. Finally, she began, "Your dad just didn't come home Friday. Nobody at the University saw him after lunchtime. He left his office at the U and never showed up for an appointment at Forst Enterprises. The police wouldn't really start looking the first day or so. I'm not sure they're very serious about it yet. They keep asking if he might have had a girlfriend!"

"Forst Enterprises?"

"Randall Forst was one of your dad's grad students years ago. He's started a very successful company making physics equipment and your dad has been working with him on some new idea of his."

Stephen stumbled sleepily down the stairs in a t-shirt and ragged shorts. He'd gotten tall! He sat down across from Allie. Then he rocked back, a stunned look on his face. "You're Eva!" Goosebumps stood up on his arms.

"No Steve, this is your sister Allie! Don't you even recognize her?"

"Your band's Eve of Destruction?"

Allie bit her lip and nodded. She hadn't considered the possibility that she might have a fan at home.

Sarah Dans looked back and forth between her two children. "Eve of Destruction?"

Allie nodded.

"Eva?"

"My stage name."

Stephen threw his head back and stared up at the ceiling. "Oh. My. GOD!" He looked back at Allie. "I must've seen your picture a million times! I can't believe that black hair fooled *me*!"

Sarah looked in wonderment at her daughter. "Even I've heard of Eve of Destruction! Why didn't you tell us you were doing well? All those calls I made offering to send you money!" She shook her head ruefully. "You really are doing OK?"

Allie grinned sheepishly and then nodded minutely.

"I guess you won't be throwing it in and coming home with your tail between your legs, to beg to go to college after all?"

Allie shrugged and shook her head.

To Allie's surprise, Sarah leaned over, threw her arms around her daughter and sobbed again. "I'm so happy for you!" she choked out.

Stephen threw his head back, thrust his arms in the air and shouted, "You're shittin' me! My sister is 'Eva?' This is awesome! Wait 'til I tell Ben."

"Stephen Dans! Watch your language!"

Allie caught her brother's eye when he looked back at her, goofy grin on his face. "Stephen, please don't tell anybody? I'd like to have a place of peace and quiet for as long as I can. Fans are important to us, but they can be pretty intrusive too."

Stephen stared wide-eyed, "You have *got* to be shittin' me! The coolest thing that's ever happened to me and I can't tell anyone?!"

"Stephen!"

Allie made calming motions with her hands. "Let's worry about that later. First we need to figure out what to do about Dad."

A pall dropped back over the table. "But what could *we* do?" Allie asked.

Sarah said, "I don't know. The police say we shouldn't do anything… just wait by the phone."

"I don't know. You've been through his desk here at home for clues?"

"Yes, and his e-mails and his hard drive. Everything in the desk and on his computer seems to be about his research on ports." Sarah's eyes cast toward Stephen then back to Allie. She shook her head minutely. Apparently they still hadn't told Stephen that Allie had been the source of the ports. "There's nothing on there about any 'other interests' either." Apparently Sarah hadn't told Stephen about the police's "girlfriend" theory either.

"What about his work computer?"

"I'm pretty sure they won't let us look at it. Besides we wouldn't have the password."

"Well, let's go try. Dad could never remember passwords. It's probably written down in his desk somewhere."

The doorbell rang again. Sarah clapped a hand to her heart, a stricken look on her face. "Oh! I hope it isn't bad news."

Allie got up. "I'll get it." A grim feeling settled over her. She strode down the hall to the entry and opened the door. Hot muggy air flowed in, followed by a scruffy, skinny young man in a white shirt and black tie. *Mormons?* she wondered, *but Mormons are polite— they wouldn't just shove into the house like this.* Then a large, wide-bodied, bald man, also in white shirt and tie came through the door as well! His dense goatee looked wrong for a Mormon. "Hey!" Allie exclaimed, as they crowded her back out of the entry and into the hallway. More words froze in her throat as she looked down at the gun in the first man's hand. *Rape?! Robbery?!* she wondered.

Dean looked at the gorgeous, slender chick with the spiky reddish blond hair. *These college girls are hot*, he thought to himself. He waved his gun at her, "You Allie?"

"Huh?" Allie said.

"We're gonna go visit your daddy and see if you can talk some sense into him."

"Put down that damned phone!" the man with the goatee roared over Allie's shoulder.

Allie looked back over her shoulder. Her mother and brother stood at the other end of the hall to the kitchen. Stephen had dropped his cell phone and it looked like it had broken.

Goatee chortled, "This is the mom and *both* kids. All right!" He was looking at a paper he'd unfolded.

"Jackpot! Let's go." He motioned back towards the door with his gun.

145

Allie thought dazedly that she'd been advised to never go anywhere with someone who meant her harm. "Stay away from environments that your abductor controls." But, "go visit your daddy," made it sound like *not* going was a poor choice too. They needed to know where her dad was.

A couple of minutes later they all stood trembling at the front door, Allie thought about running as soon as they were out in public, she'd read somewhere that that was a good strategy. Grabbing her hand, Goatee said, "Let's hold hands so you don't get any ideas." Then he squeezed painfully until Allie dropped to her knees. He said in an ominous tone, "We really only need one of you three to convince your old man to talk. So if one of you kids runs, or gives us any other trouble, we'll *kill* the old lady. Think about that long and hard before you decide to take off."

Allie looked up into Goatee's pale blue eyes and could see that he enjoyed hurting her. Tears welled up and she looked back down and shook her head. Should she make a port in his neck like that guy at the bar? It didn't seem like a good idea to make him cough while she was looking down the barrel of his gun.

Dean grinned at the way Roger hurt the chica. He and Roger had that in common; they both liked to hurt people. They couldn't afford to have her run, which provided a convenient excuse. He opened the front door and, putting away his gun, started down the walk, opening the door to the back of the van for their guests and then locking them into the windowless, dim interior with Roger. Roger got out blindfolds. Dean went around front, got in, started the van, and eased it into the street. He took a random course across town with a couple of loop backs looking for tails. About an hour later they pulled up at the little farmhouse where the boss was holding daddy Dans.

146

Since they had the blindfolds on, Roger took Allie's arm and led her up the walk. Dean got the other two out of the back, but then paused to watch the girl's cute looking ass as it swayed going up the steps. Once that was over he started the mom and brother up the walk too.

Allie was pulled up a few steps, then heard the creak of a door. She felt a puff of cool air and then felt Goatee's hand on her elbow urging her up over a sill into a dim room. The blindfold was removed and she saw a man tied to a chair. Her dad! Face swollen, and nose crooked, but it was definitely him. Allie ran to him, dropping to her knees and throwing her arms around him. "Daddy," she whispered.

"Allie!" A happy-to-see-you emotion bloomed in her dad's eyes. After a moment he mumbled through swollen lips, "Sorry kiddo. Seems like I really screwed up."

Then Goatee hauled Allie back by the belt and tossed her against the wall. Effortlessly, it seemed.

Allie lay stunned. She heard her mother screaming hysterically as if from far away. She looked up blurrily to see Stephen charge over to tackle Goatee, but Goatee clubbed him aside with his gun, using a vicious stroke that left the young teenager lying, apparently unconscious, against the other wall. This assault on her brother shocked Allie's mind clear, but it still seemed like she couldn't move.

Scruffy pulled out some cable ties and tossed some to Goatee. They started methodically tying up Allie's mother, apparently unfazed by her struggles and shrieks. Goatee simply held her arms still while Scruffy fastened her wrists and elbows to the arms of the wooden chair with the cable ties. Then they did the same thing with her ankles and knees.

Allie could see that Stephen was still breathing. Though her brother still appeared to be unconscious, they bound his ankles and wrists together. But not Allie, which somehow seemed ominous. Then they turned back to Mrs. Dans who was still yelling at the top of her lungs. Goatee slapped her hard. When this stopped her yelling for a moment, he said, "Shut up unless you want to be gagged." He gave her an ugly smile, "People *can* choke to death on gags you know."

Allie heard a new and raspy voice, "Purdy thing, ain't she?" Raspy, Allie saw, had white hair and a face pitted with old acne scars. He held a gun casually pointed halfway between Allie and her dad. He took a long drag from a cigarette and blew a stream of smoke towards her. From the lazy, casual way he held the gun she got the distinct impression that he'd killed people with it.

Raspy turned to her dad, "Now, Dr. Dans, I *sure* would hate to see your purdy daughter hurt just 'cause you want to keep your little ol' secret all to yourself."

*Dad has secrets?* Allie thought with some startlement. What kind of secret would he have that would involve this kind of people? They'd always been comfortably well off, though not rich—could he be involved in some kind of crime? Wouldn't she have had some kind of hint before now? He was a physicist! She thought? Physicists didn't have secrets! Did they? She shuffled herself into a sitting position against the wall. It made her head swim, but she didn't want to be lying down in this situation.

Muzzily, she pondered their situation. It seemed pretty grim with everyone tied up but her. She had a sick feeling that even if her dad parted with his secrets, the family wouldn't be leaving here alive. Every member of the family had seen the men's faces, so the men would be crazy to let them go to the police afterward.

Lazily, Raspy pointed the gun toward Allie. There was a flash, a loud bang and Allie let out a brief shriek and

148

scrunched in on herself. Bits of sheetrock dribbled down the wall onto her head. She stared at the gun like it was a snake. Raspy'd been talking she realized, "Don't worry little lady, you can scream all you want. No one'll hear you out here. Go ahead and holler to your heart's content. Maybe it'll motivate your old man here. You need to get him talking before I have to actually start shooting parts of you. Parts is parts ya know?" He chuckled as if he'd said something very funny.

"What do you need to know? My dad doesn't have any secrets."

Raspy barked a short laugh. "Oh, Doc, even your kids don't know? Well Honey, it seems your Daddy developed a wormhole device, but he doesn't want to share his secret with the world."

Startled, Allie looked at her dad questioningly. He shook his head minutely. For a moment she didn't comprehend, then she realized with awe that, even after the beating he'd apparently taken, he still hadn't told them that *she'd* created the ports!

Allie's dad croaked, "I've *told* them the ports are too small to be useful!"

Raspy casually backhanded her dad with the pistol, knocking him, and the chair he was tied to, over onto their sides. The gunsight cut the side of his head leaving a long bleeding gash over his ear. "Dans, I really am tired of hearing you talk, *without* telling us what we need to know, so shut up! *We're* gonna have some fun with your little girl here, but it'll stop anytime you want to start talking about things we *want* to know. Understand?"

Goatee had easily picked up the chair Allie's dad was strapped to, setting it and him back upright. Her dad mumbled something.

"What?!"

Her dad said, "I said, 'Just kill us all. You're going to anyway.'"

149

Raspy snorted, "Well now, it might come to that. But first we'll have some fun eh? Dean, you evil bastard, you wanna have some fun with the chica there?"

Dean, licked his lips and swaggered over to the girl, expecting to enjoy the apprehensive look on her face. Instead she looked pissed. Oh well. Then he tilted his head and looked at her again. "A-hah! I've been thinking there was something kinda familiar about you. It's 'cause you look like a redheaded version of Eva, you know, the singer from Eve of Destruction?" He grabbed her arm and hauled her to her feet, groping her on the way up.

He grunted and crouched over in pain. *Damn! The bitch kneed me in the crotch!* As soon as he recovered a little, he slapped her brutally and watched with satisfaction as she crumpled to the floor. He bent back over, holding his knees and grunted, "Roger, looks like I'm gonna need a little help."

"Sure thing buddy." Roger said, picking a stunned Allie up by one arm and her belt and carrying her to the heavy dining table.

Dean huffed a couple of times, then stood a little straighter and walked over to the can of cable ties. Roger tossed Allie onto the heavy table and held her while Dean tied her ankles and wrists.

Allie raised up her spinning head and saw her father looking on in horror. Her mother started screaming, but that choked off to muffled sobs as they gagged her after all. Allie looked around the room. Her brother still lay unmoving, though she could see he was still breathing. *Could I do something besides make these bastards cough? Are there others? Or just Raspy, Scruffy, and Goatee?* She didn't want to try making them cough themselves senseless when someone might pop out of the other room with a gun.

Dean reached out and grabbed her chin forcing her to look at him, "Kick me *now*, bitch."

Allie tried to twist her face away from his hand, but it was futile.

Leering over her, he said, "I'm gonna pretend I'm screwing that rock star, Eva. You *look* like her and she's probably an uppity bitch just like you are."

She focused and could feel the blood vessels in his groin. With trepidation she focused on the big artery there and created a port from there to his pants. A bloody spot appeared near his crotch.

Roger guffawed, pointing at Dean's crotch, "Hey buddy, she rupture something there when she kicked ya?

Dean looked down and began a panicked cursing.

Out of the corner of her eye Allie saw Raspy getting up to look. After a moment, Raspy calmly told Dean to change his pants, wash up and figure out what was bleeding. Dean went into the bathroom to desperately examine himself for the source of bleeding, swearing all the while. Roger and Raspy chuckled at Dean's condition, even though they were obviously a little spooked themselves.

Allie looked up apprehensively as Roger stepped up beside her. He grinned, but the expression looked evil on him. "I guess it's just you and me, Cutie." He said, reaching out, "I like to choke cute girls like you," he said, raising his eyebrows as if she were supposed to be amazed by this revelation. He grasped her neck and started squeezing.

Allie gasped for breath as his grip slowly tightened. Her mother was screaming into her gag and Allie heard a crash as her Dad's chair fell over. She thrashed to try to get free without success, Roger was far too strong. His face was flushed, the veins standing out. He was excited and dangerous, she concluded, and she was going to be unconscious soon. She couldn't wait any longer to be sure whether there were other accomplices or to think of some better strategy. Reaching out with her odd sense she felt the pulsating arteries in his neck and the flow of air in his windpipe. Allie created a port from his carotid artery into to his trachea and Roger suddenly let go of her neck as he began spasmodically coughing up blood just like the big drunk behind the bar. Raspy hove into view desperately waving his gun in all directions, shouting, "What the *hell* just happened Roger?!"

Through a bloody moustache and goatee Roger gasped out, "Don't... *cough, cough*... know!" then resumed hacking.

Raspy pointed the gun at Allie's leg, "Step into view or I put a bullet in the girl's leg!" When nothing happened, he said, "Now!"

Allie realized that Raspy thought her family had an accomplice. She didn't want to make him spasm with coughing; he might pull the trigger when she did. While she dithered Allie saw his finger tighten on the trigger. Desperately she tried to twist her leg out of the way. He used his left hand to hold her leg down, then pulled the trigger!

Agony scythed through Allie's calf. She tried to reach out and sense Raspy's neck, but found that her tele-sense couldn't feel anything while her leg was hurting so badly! She curled up and grasped at her leg with her hands, though she had difficulty doing it with her wrists bound together. It seemed like the bullet had missed the bone as her leg wasn't flopping around. The hole was in the fleshy part of her calf, but it still hurt terribly. She had to do something about their guns!

Raspy continued waving his gun about, but seemed less frantic as nothing had happened after he shot Allie. Roger's coughing had died down, though he still bent over and braced against his knees. Dean came back into the room from the bathroom wearing new shorts, but no shoes. He waved his gun around too, but both he and Raspy slowly became calmer when nothing else happened.

Allie's pain diminished to a dull throb and she sent her sense into her leg. Nothing broken, the bullet had gone in the front and out the back between the bones. With a sudden idea, Allie reached out with her sense and found the water pipe in the kitchen wall right behind her. She focused on Raspy's gun, feeling the bullet in the chamber, then the powder in the shell behind the bullet. She opened a tiny port and was rewarded by the sensation of water spraying into the powder. Was it enough? She worried that if she opened the port too far, the water pressure might push the bullet out of the end of the cartridge and she surely didn't want water dripping out of the gun to warn them that something was wrong. With a mental shrug, she turned to the gun that Dean had stopped waving and put back in his waistband holster, then to the one in Roger's holster wetting them all. She considered wetting the powder in the second cartridge in each gun, in case they just jacked the slide if the first bullet didn't fire. Her leg was throbbing and she was finding it harder to concentrate and sense the water pipe so she closed her eyes for a moment's rest. *There must be something better she could do!*

Allie's dad croaked, "If you'll just let my family go, I'll show you how I made the first device."

Raspy chuckled, "Oh sure, that's a good one! You betcha Albert, you just promise, cross your heart, hope to die and we'll let the family go to the police while you're 'splainin' how to make the port machine. Sho' 'nuff Albert, tha'd be jes' fine!" He laughed some more. There was a grunt and scraping of chair legs as he set the chair Dr. Dans was tied to back up right. "Oopsie, no, *that* wouldn't work! Instead why don't you start explaining and drawing pictures of the device right now, just so's I *won't* put any more bullets into your daughter?"

"OK, but first put a bandage on her leg and take the gag off my wife."

"We'll bandage the girl's leg, but your wife makes too much noise. I ain't takin' that gag off."

"OK, but you've got to let one of us check on Stephen."

Allie felt surprised that her dad appeared to be negotiating in such a level headed fashion. He'd always seemed brilliant, in an absent-minded, nebulous sort of way. Far too fuzzy headed for this type of negotiation.

Someone started cutting her pants leg open. She opened her eyes and saw Dean cutting them with a knife. Allie looked over at her dad. Her dad gave her a little half wink! He must realize what had caused the storm of coughing? She looked at the small wound on her calf, the entrance, she presumed. The exit wound would be around back. They weren't bleeding much. She wiggled her foot. It hurt, but the muscles worked. Dean said, "Hell, she ain't hurt." But he cut her pants leg into strips and wrapped them around her calf anyway.

"Let me check my brother," Allie said.

Raspy said, "Soon as your dad starts drawing."

Allie looked and saw that Roger had lifted her dad's chair and put it next to the table. They cut her dad's hands loose and shoved paper and pencil in front of him. Her dad stared at Allie with a look of concentration as if he was trying to tell her something, but she had no idea what. Then he pulled the paper to himself and started drawing.

Dean cut Allie's hands, then her feet loose, then stepped back and pointed his gun at her. Allie swung her legs off the table and stood gingerly. Her leg hurt, but not horribly. *Best not to let on though.*

Playing her injury up, she limped and stumbled over to Stephen and crouched down. He was still breathing and had a strong pulse but didn't respond when she said his name. She pulled back an eyelid because she knew that's what medical people did, but she had no idea what to look for. So she reached out with her strange sense to feel the inside of his head. She wondered what his brain was supposed to feel like, never having done this before. The left side was different than the right! *Crap, was it supposed to be that way?* There was an area between the skull and what Allie assumed must be his brain on the left side that seemed different. She realized the pressure was higher there! She'd heard of people bleeding into their heads and knew that such bleeding was bad! Her first impulse was to demand that they take Stephen to a hospital, but she knew that would *never* happen. Could she let out the pressure? What if she did some harm? Her thoughts raced desperately, but after a moment she decided she was pretty sure he *was* going to die if she *didn't* do anything!

Allie gritted her teeth and formed a port from the area of high pressure inside his skull, to the outside of his head. She was immediately relieved to see blood staining his hair, indicating she wasn't letting grey matter leak out. At least she didn't *think* it was grey matter. She ran her fingers through it to be sure there wasn't any brain in the stuff leaking out and was relieved to find only blood. She looked up and saw her mother's wide eyes; her dad just looked grim at the sight of the blood on her fingers. She looked back down at Stephen and let more blood out until the pressure was low enough that it didn't flow any more. By the time she'd finished doing that she had a headache and knew she wouldn't be able to make more than a tiny port for a while. She hoped that the bleeding in his head had stopped.

Raspy said, "Keep drawing!"

155

Allie looked back over at her dad and saw him look back down from her and focus on whatever he was drawing.

Allie sat down next to Stephen and tried to look non-threatening so that they wouldn't tie her back up. For a moment, she wondered what her dad was actually drawing and what they would do when they found out it wasn't really a port producing machine. She put her head back and closed her eyes as if exhausted, which she actually was. If she were to make these guys bleed into their skulls like Stephen had, how long would it take them to become unconscious? Her leg was hurting in this position, she reached down and grasped her thigh to move it.

Her hand struck a lump in the pocket of her baggy cargo jeans. Her little tube of Mace pepper spray! She restrained the impulse to whoop and instead considered how to use it? She needed to wait a while because right now she would be limited in her ability to make ports. She just rested her head back on the wall with one hand on Stephen's neck and closed her eyes. She needed some way to deal with these guys one at a time. But how…?

Stephen moved under Allie's hand and she was startled to realize that she was so exhausted that she'd actually dozed off! She looked down at her brother. His eyes were open! He looked muzzy headed and unfocused, but he was awake! "Stephen," she bent over him, "you got hit on the head and you're just waking up." Allie sensed that a little blood had reaccumulated, though it wasn't much. She drained it out anyway. She looked over at her parents.

"Stephen's awake! Still looks pretty stunned though." She turned to Raspy, "We need to get him to a hospital."

"Sure, Honey. Soon's your dad finishes his drawings and explanations, we'll be on our way."

From the smirk on Raspy's face she could tell that it *wasn't* going to happen. She thought for a few more moments and decided that things probably wouldn't get better. She was untied and at least her dad's hands were free. "I've gotta pee," she said as plaintively as she could.

Raspy looked up from where he was watching Dr. Dans draw. He caught Dean's eye and jerked a thumb over his shoulder.

Dean waved her to her feet with his gun and she limped across the living room area to the hallway where she presumed the bathroom was. Just down the hall an open door revealed a dirty bathroom. She stepped inside and started to close the door but to her startlement Dean blocked the door with his foot. "Nah, I gotta be with you," he said with a nasty grin.

At first Allie was dismayed to have this man in the bathroom with her but then realized that this played right into her intentions. She said, "OK, but you gotta turn your back."

"Sure," he snickered and faced into the corner. Allie thought he probably planned to peek into the mirror on the back of the door or something so she did pull down her pants and sat on the toilet. Then she reached out with her odd sense for the cold water pipe under the sink and also for Dean's skull. She aligned the port to face toward his skull so that the spray of water wouldn't cut into the soft matter of his brain, then opened a port as big as she could. She'd heard that the brain didn't have any sensory nerves in it, but Dean must have felt the vibration of the spray right through his skull because he reached tentatively up to the side of his head. But a moment later he made a little grunting sound, swayed and started to fall over backward. Allie scrambled up from the toilet and caught him before he crashed to the floor. She laid him down gently, then sat back down and peed because she really did have to go. She flushed the

157

toilet, washed her hands and went back out to the living room, glancing at the closed bedroom doors on her way. She wondered if there was someone else in one of the bedrooms, then she saw a tiny TV camera up in the corner of the hall. Probably, she decided. Someone monitoring things on the camera.

Raspy grunted and said, "Where's Dean?"

Allie shrugged, "He had to pee too." She noticed that Stephen had rolled over and thought that must be a good sign. Allie's mother was watching her intently, and as Allie looked at her, Sarah's eyes flicked over at Roger where he sat on the couch, picking his nose.

Allie's dad cleared his throat, "Do you want me to explain the drawings I've made so far to you? Or should I wait to explain them to Randy?"

Raspy said, "To Mr. Forst?" He glanced up at the light fixture over the table where Allie recognized the lens of another camera. Raspy looked back down at the drawing, "Naw, you can explain it to me."

Her dad started talking and pointing to things on the drawing, but Allie tuned him out and focused on the pipe in the kitchen wall and on the inside of Roger's skull. Once she was sure of her locations, she again opened as big a port as she could. Roger looked puzzled and also reached up to the side of his head. Allie was finding that it was difficult to hold this port open, but she strained to do so for a few moments longer until she saw Roger slumping and making convulsive swallowing movements. Then his head flopped back and he started to snore. Loudly! Allie gasped as she let the port drop shut.

Raspy turned to look at his compatriot who was now slumping to the side and drooling as he snorted another breath. "Roger! You idiot! Wake up!"

When Roger didn't move, Raspy's eyes opened wide and he stepped over and kicked Roger's leg. "Roger!" The big man just sagged farther to the side and Raspy pulled out his gun with startling swiftness.

"Dean! Get your butt in here!" Allie knew she didn't have the strength to make another port big enough and long enough to put Raspy out too! Raspy was looking wildly around the room as if suspecting someone of shooting poisoned darts or something. Worse, he was moving around constantly, presumably to avoid such darts, but also making it hard for Allie to consider making a port inside Raspy in precisely the right location. Raspy suddenly shouted, "Come out you bastard or I kill the kid!" He pointed his gun at Stephen!

Allie panicked, any of the things she could think to do might make him pull the trigger and she thought she would only be able to make a little port. She focused on the inside of her Mace pepper spray cartridge, then reached out for Raspy's nasal passages. Could she grab the gun and make a port at the same time? Suddenly, off to Raspy's left she saw her mother tip her chair over. The sudden motion and loud bang as the chair hit the floor caused Raspy to move the gun briefly towards Mrs. Dans. As it did, Allie opened the biggest port she could from the Mace canister to the back of Raspy's nasal passage. She immediately knew it was a small port, but apparently it was plenty big enough to let a significant dose of capsaicin through.

Raspy threw his head back in agony. Allie saw him convulsively squeeze the trigger. The gun was pointing at Stephen again! There was a little pop, like a cap gun, but no roar.

Damn! She'd forgotten that she'd let water into that cartridge. Raspy fell to his knees and dropped the gun, clutching his face which had turned bright red. He was coughing and gasping for breath and tears were pouring down his cheeks. Allie picked up the gun and jacked the slide to get the wet bullet out of the chamber. Then she handed the gun to her dad and went to get the knife out of the holster on Roger's belt.

Allie had just started cutting her mother's gag loose when one of the bedroom doors slammed open and a man stepped into the room carrying a sawed off shotgun. "Dans, put that phone down!" he yelled.

Allie saw her dad had a phone in his hand. Apparently he'd picked it up off the end table behind him. He dropped it on the floor. "Hello Forst," he said resignedly.

"So Dans, I'm thinking your daughter has the port machine somewhere in those baggy ass pants."

When Allie started to move to her mother again Forst shouted, "Keep your hands up kid!"

Allie found herself looking down the apparently huge barrel of the shotgun and she slowly raised her hands in the air.

"What are you doing with a knife?"

"Cutting my mom loose."

"Ah. Well. Put the knife on the table and step over here into the middle of the room. Humpf, to think your dad had a working model all this time and yet he had me chasing my tail trying to make another!"

Allie slowly set the knife on the table. She tried to reach out with her sense for the shell in the chamber of the shotgun, but it seemed like she'd exhausted her talent for the moment. She stepped over to where he indicated.

"Now, I want you to take off those pants without reaching in the pockets. I don't know how you control the 'porter', but I don't want your hands even getting near it. If I even *think* you're trying to do so, I will fire this shotgun, got that? I'll shoot you above the waist though." He chuckled. "Wouldn't want to damage the porter!"

Allie nodded and slowly reached for her belt, loosening it and the snap to her pants, then letting the loose pants fall.

Forst stared at her for a moment. "Nice legs! Now kick the pants over here. I don't suppose you'd tell me what you did to these idiots I've got working for me?" He pointed with his chin to Raspy, still wiping at his eyes and struggling to breathe on the floor.

Allie again tried to sense the shell in the shotgun, to no avail. She stepped out of the pants and kicked them over part of the way to Forst.

Still looking at her legs, he stepped forward, reaching down for the pants. As he did so, the barrel of the shotgun dipped toward the floor! Could she grab it? She was starting to step forward when, BANG! BANG! BANG! BANG! Forst was thrown against the wall. Allie looked over to see her dad lowering Raspy's smoking gun. In the sudden ringing silence, "Holy crap, Dad! I didn't know you could shoot!"

"Actually a gun's a pretty simple tool." He reached onto the table and picked up the knife, cutting his ankles loose from the chair.

Allie stepped over to check on Forst who was still breathing but had four holes in his torso and looked to be in pretty bad shape. "We'd better call 911."

Her dad nodded at the phone where it lay on the floor, "They're still on the line, I'm sure they'll be here pronto after hearing gunshots." Now he was cutting his wife loose from her chair. "Put Forst's head down and his legs up, then check on your brother again if you can." In a whisper he asked, "You drained a hematoma off Stephen's brain?"

Assuming he didn't want the 911 people to hear she whispered back, "There was a collection of blood next to his brain that I let out, yes. Is that a 'hematoma'?"

"Yep, good thinking. Did you bleed these other guys into their heads too?" He was checking on Roger and laying him down on the couch.

"No, just cold water out of a pipe."

Allie pulled Forst around until his head was on the floor, then lifted his feet up onto a chair.

161

Allie's mom picked the phone up off the floor and listened for a moment. "Yes there's been a shooting and several people are badly hurt. Please hurry! No, the shooting's all over and the… kidnappers have been disarmed. Please hurry."

Her dad turned to her, not seeming at all like his usual absent minded self. In a low voice, "OK, we don't want the police figuring out what you can do, how did you keep the gun from shooting Stephen?"

"Water in the cartridge."

Her dad nodded. "Find the shell you jacked out of the chamber. Did you do that to any of the other shells?"

Allie nodded, "First shell in each of their guns." She was astonished at how fast her dad was figuring all this out. He didn't seem at all like the doddering, befuddled professor she thought she knew.

"OK and put your pants back on." He headed into the kitchen and came back with a dish towel.

Startled to realize that she was still just wearing her panties, Allie put her pants back on and picked up the shell off the floor. Her dad came back from the bathroom with another cartridge and went to Mrs. Dans, gently placing her hand over the mouthpiece of the phone. He started talking while he went to Roger, pulling his gun out of his shoulder holster with the dishtowel and jacking the slide, then putting the gun back without touching it with his fingers. He was saying, "Here's our story, 'Dean and Roger got in a fight in the bathroom and Dean never came back out. Roger must have gotten hurt because he passed out after he came back in here; Allie shot Jones with her pepper spray when he threatened to shoot Stephen. Otherwise we tell the truth about how they were trying to beat a technical secret out of me and threatening you to obtain my cooperation. The fewer the lies, the better our story will hold together."

Allie realized that Jones must be Raspy's real name. She bent close to her brother and sensed the inside of his skull. There was a little bit of blood but it didn't seem like much and there wasn't any pressure so, as weak as her port ability was, she didn't try to let any out. She looked over at her mom who was calmly telling the 911 people that there were three unconscious people and one "bad" man who'd been shot. She heard the water running in the kitchen. The door slammed open and two armored, helmeted policemen burst in wielding shotguns, "Hands up!" Allie and her mom put their hands up. Her dad called out, "I'm coming out of the kitchen." After an OK from the policeman he stepped out of the kitchen with his hands up too.

Allie rode in the ambulance with Stephen and her dad. Stephen was admitted to the hospital and taken away for a CAT scan. They x-rayed Allie's leg in the ED, gave her some antibiotics and turned Allie and her dad back over to the police for questioning. X-rays had shown that Dr. Dans' nose was broken, but they taped a splint over it and set him up to straighten it the next day. Her mother had already been questioned and released back to stay with Stephen. At the police station, Allie and her dad were questioned for about an hour or so and then they took a taxi back to the hospital to find that Stephen was sitting up and talking, though still a little confused about what had happened.
Later as they went down to the hospital cafeteria, Allie's dad said, "I want you to know how very proud I am of you, Allie. It amazed me how you kept your cool when you were dealing with those guys."
She tilted her head, and narrowed her eyes, "You aren't mad that I didn't tell you I could make ports again?"

He chuckled, "No. I've always thought you probably could do it, but just didn't want to because I was such a pest. I think I deserved it. And now I can see that a port has terrible potential as a weapon, not just as a useful technology." He got a wistful look on his face, but then turned to look her in the eyes. "I guess I'll give up on it." He paused, then said, "I also wanted to tell you how wonderful I think your success with 'Eve of Destruction' is. You have *two* amazing talents and personally, I think your music is astonishing."

Allie and her mom both stopped in their tracks.

Her mom said, "You knew?!"

Allie said, "You've listened to our music?!"

He shrugged, "Sure, I've got both CDs and I went to two of your concerts when I was in Buffalo for a meeting last summer. It felt really cool, being in that crowd, knowing *I* was 'Eva's' dad."

Allie's mom said plaintively, "And you didn't tell me?"

"You didn't know? And here I thought *I* was the oblivious one."

### The End

What if - you could open wormholes from one location to another with your mind?

## BILLY BENOIT

Billy Benoit had been transmuted.
A change apparent at first glance to anyone who'd known him, even as casually as I had. Not transmuted as lead into gold, but more as brass into iron. Rusty, worn, beaten, or perhaps just hammered iron, but iron nonetheless. Hair still dark; handsome face still unwrinkled; frame still slender, yet muscular; but now age and experience hung about him like an aura.
I had just entered Joel's Hole as was my habit of a Friday night—after a week at the desk—to drink a few beers, to shoot the proverbial shit, and to hope that some woman would pick me up and take me home. Since I almost never had the courage to try to pick up a woman myself, I relied on an occasional desperate woman who might make the first move on me.
Regularly, at some point during most evenings at Joel's, I had a brief, backslapping, chest-puffing conversation with Billy. An exchange usually inspired by a desire to get closer to Billy's companion. He would be there with a different woman almost every Friday, usually recently met, almost always the most attractive girl in the club.
Billy and I would exchange a few meaningless pleasantries in the fashion of men, mostly braggadocios and insults. Eventually he would introduce me to his new lady and shortly after that I would move on. Later I would observe with envy as they became more and more entwined until eventually he maneuvered her out the door—low purpose in mind.
But the night that I saw Billy had changed, I found him alone. His solitary status alone was exceptional, but, ignoring that, there was still a distinction. It *was* him, but it wasn't the *familiar* him. Curious, I found myself

165

settling onto the adjacent stool. Not to spend a few minutes on meaningless trivialities as had been our custom, but already cognizant somehow, that I would be there for hours.

"What happened?" I asked.

As he turned to face me, there was no surprise on his face. No question in his eyes that I would *know* something had changed in him. His stare was penetrating as he said, "You write, don't you?"

Neither Billy nor I had ever, to my recollection, spoken of our work, so the question surprised me. Mildly taken aback, I said, "Well I write some, more of a hobby. I've never had anything commercially published, but I must have converted at least *one* tree into rejection slips."

It was a poor joke, but one repeated often enough that my polished delivery usually brought at least a smirk.

No smirks this time.

Billy continued sizing me up for another few seconds and then said quietly, "I'll tell *you* a story."

I've cursed myself several times since that night for not insisting on recording his tale. Of course, I didn't think I'd hear much of a story. Other, closer, friends had told me yarns that they thought ought to be written; those stories had *all* been crap. So it wasn't 'til we were deep into his tale that I found myself expecting that, of course, I would try to write *this* story out.

But, not wanting to interrupt Billy, I just let him ramble on. I figured that I'd just catch him later for any poorly recalled details.

I haven't seen Billy since.


He began the story by reminding me that we'd met in our usual fashion the Friday before. He'd accompanied an exquisite blond woman named Kim. I'd stopped by to be introduced, to ogle Kim, and told them a few bad jokes. To my shame, I admit that all I actually remember of Kim was her cleavage. Despite her quirked smile of amusement over my attraction to it, that cleavage repeatedly drew my eyes—kind of like moths banging into a light.

Billy related that after my departure he'd been surprised to find himself having an actual *conversation* with Kim. Certainly, he spoke to all the ladies he spent time with, but those were mere chats about meaningless trivialities. With Kim he found himself actually listening and arguing. Rather than merely trying to impress a girl with his conversational talent, he found himself wanting to know what *she* thought about the topics.

She had an odd perspective on life, as if she were from a foreign country, though she had no accent. She questioned concepts that Billy accepted as matters of fact, especially things historical. As she would disagree with Billy's prejudice on an issue, she would repeatedly point out that history is written by the winners. They spoke of literature, famous writers, and science fiction.

At one point, Billy said, the topic ran aground upon Mark Twain's "A Connecticut Yankee." Billy's contention had focused on his feeling that it would be *great* to go back in time where he, with his modern knowledge, could "kick ass and take names."

She'd disagreed. She felt that even "simple" technology required significant "pre-existing art" and necessitated a certain knowledge and technology base. The combination of skills required by the "Yankee" just didn't exist in a single, unaided human. She said, "Even if you knew that gunpowder needed saltpeter, you probably wouldn't know what saltpeter actually was, where it could be found, or how it could be purified".

Billy allowed that the "Yankee" had accomplished more than most people could, but still felt that he, Billy

Benoit, "would be king of the mountain in no time," especially if he was to go back even further in time. Far enough back that he could invent the bow and arrow or domesticate the horse.

To Billy's surprise Kim turned out to be a willing bed partner that night and even more to his amazement they returned to argue the "Yankee" concept after sex, but before sleep. During their contention her eyes flashed with merriment and he had the constant feeling she was laughing *at* him, rather than *with* him.

Billy woke the next morning with a throbbing pain in his jaw. It was cold. He was gnawingly hungry and sore all over. His tongue probed and found swollen, inflamed gums about a molar that was partly gone. His breasts were sore.

Breasts!

To his horror, he realized that during the night he'd become a woman!

A woman who called herself Teba. Billy and Teba were cohabiting "her" body. He found with some astonishment that he was *not* surprised to be sharing this woman's body. He "knew" with a certain conviction that Kim had sent him back in time by placing him in Teba's mind and realized simultaneously and with complete confidence that Kim had been visiting us from our own future.

Teba didn't find it unusual to have a throbbing tooth in her jaw. It had been throbbing for weeks now. Teba wasn't surprised to be hungry either. There had been nothing but a few roots to eat yesterday and the tribe had only had a rabbit to share the day before. The general soreness of her body went practically unnoticed by Teba. It came from sleeping on a thin layer of rotting leaves over a surface of cold hard dirt. She was in a cave of sorts, lying in a mass of tangled limbs with the other fourteen members of her tribe.

They were huddled together for warmth. The "cave" was in reality just a place with a rock overhang big enough to provide some shelter. Its mouth was too large to really close out the weather.

Teba began extricating herself from the surrounding bodies with an urge to empty her bladder. Billy, though he sensed that he was ultimately in control, felt so stunned by his new circumstances that he was perfectly willing to let Teba move about her usual morning functions without his interference. Teba moved with great care lest she disturb the others, especially the five men, whom, Billy recognized with surprise, she uniformly dreaded and feared.

Once up, she went out into the cold to perch on the end of a nearby log which overhung a foul smelling mess of human offal. A glance told Billy that it would smell much worse when things warmed up. Although the morning bordered on frosty, Teba felt pleased that it seemed a little warmer than mornings had been. She looked forward to the near future with *eager* anticipation of a full belly.

Billy recognized, after pondering Teba's memories, that spring must be coming soon and that winter had always meant a scarcity of game with long stretches of hunger. Billy's mind began to look forward to the changes he was going to make—a little modern day knowledge was going to go *much* farther in caveman times than it had in the old England of the Connecticut Yankee!

When Teba returned to the cave others had begun stirring. Her stomach turned. Bant was awake and staring at her! Muscular, squat, easily-angered, brutal Bant. To her relief he quickly shuffled out of the cave toward the "log." Teba ruffled her son Gano's hair and hugged him briefly, wishing she had something to feed him.

Billy felt Teba's fear and knew that it had to do with Bant's constant desire for sex. Billy discerned his own queasy revulsion over the possibility of being on the receiving end of the sex act and yet felt a tingling curiosity about what it would be like as a woman. Suddenly a lancing pain came from Teba's scalp. She was forced to her knees by a powerful grip on her hair. Billy felt her dropping quickly, utterly resigned to the inevitability of the act. She bent forward. Shocked initially at the brutality of it, Billy suddenly raged at the thought that this was being done *to* him. He hadn't given his consent!

Rape was something Billy had given little thought to as a man. Now, in Teba's mind he learned that it was the only form of sex she'd ever known. In fact she thought of rape as an inevitable fact of a woman's existence.

Furious, Billy decided that it was time to start teaching these "cavemen" that the general order of things had just changed. He'd had a little self-defense course once and surely knew more about fighting than this brute behind him! Teba's mind registered consternation as Billy took over, rolling her to her side, then onto her back. He lashed out with her right foot. It smashed into Bant's crotch with a satisfying crunch.

Bant's eyes flashed wide in anger, but then he dropped to his own knees as pain radiated in waves from his groin and took his breath away. Teba scrambled to her feet, desperately wanting to apologize. Billy stopped her before her first word came out, puzzled in some sense to realize that these people had a language, but not surprised that he understood their language through Teba. Billy felt aware of the gibbering terror pouring through Teba, but didn't worry himself.

Further, he recognized the astonished wrath on the face of Bant as the man began to rise to his feet. "There's more where that came from, Bant," Billy had Teba say.

Teba was absolutely panicked by the words that had just crossed her lips.

Bant looked startled. Then he simply stepped across the intervening two paces and drove his fist into Teba's abdomen with astonishing force. Teba/Billy dropped to the ground as if his/her strings had been cut. Billy couldn't believe the power of the blow Bant had just delivered.

Unable to breath or really even to move, Teba reflexively covered her head with her arms against the rain of kicks and blows she knew would, and did, come. As Teba/Billy lay in agony under the seemingly endless battering, desperate to get his/her breath, Teba was astounded at "their" temerity in resisting Bant.

To Teba's horror, Gano darted forward to attack Bant in an effort to stop the man's assault on Gano's mother. Bant knocked the boy aside with a blow that seemed like an afterthought, but left Gano curled miserably on his side.

Billy, for his part, felt bewildered by the pitiful ease with which Bant's single crushing blow had defeated them. There had been no dancing about, no feints, no trial punches, and no time for Billy to finesse victory with some exciting martial arts move.

A martial arts move which he began to realize he might have seen on TV, but didn't really know how to execute. He'd heard someone say once that *real* fights ended in just one or two blows.

Now he understood why.

One blow from Bant and he'd found himself lying puddled on the ground, gasping to breathe. When the blows stopped, Bant wrapped his hand in Teba's hair. The man dragged Teba/Billy to her/his knees and *then* Billy found out first hand *exactly* what being raped felt like. When he'd finished, Bant followed up with another brief beating, then left Teba/Billy sobbing on the floor of the cave.

Teba crawled over to her son and huddled around him, trying to comfort the boy.

Bant and the other men collected their gear and left on a hunt.

As soon as the men were gone, Selah, the tribe's mother figure, came over and lifted Teba's head into her lap. Billy expected her to apologize for not trying to intervene. Instead, stroking Teba's head gently she asked, "Teba, what came over you?! Have you been possessed by a demon spirit?"

Teba's mind, still gibbering, indeed thought of herself as possessed by a demon, but Billy forcefully suppressed her attempt at communication on that issue. Instead he focused bitterly on his anticipation of their revenge on Bant.

As the pain began to ease, Billy set himself to ransacking Teba's memory for information on the tribe's level of technology. She knew little of their hunting or weapons. They used spears tipped with whatever sharp objects were to hand; including bone fragments, broken stones and simple fire hardening of the wooden points. Teba had witnessed only one hunt. In that one, the hunters had surrounded a sickly animal and stabbed it to death. She had no recollection of spear throwing, nor knowledge of other hunting techniques. Teba had seen the men breaking stones to try to obtain points. Billy realized with chagrin that he had no idea what flint looked like and so, though he had Teba's memories of the stone that the men had broken, he didn't know *whether* it was flint, nor how he would teach them to find flint if it wasn't.

The tribe used fire, but apparently couldn't start a fire if it burned out. It would appear from Teba's memories that they hadn't had a fire for the entire past winter because it had burned out shortly after the weather got cold. *Aha,* Billy thought to himself, *I can build a fire!*

172

*But, first I need a weapon to dispatch Bant.*
As Billy began picturing Bant with a spear or knife in his side, to his surprise Teba became terribly distraught. It became apparent that if Billy/Teba seriously injured Bant she thought it would be a horrible blow to the tribe as a whole. Without Bant, Teba didn't think there would be enough food to eat. Despite her fear of Bant and her primeval dislike for the man, she had an instinctive conviction that the tribe needed *all* its hunters if they were to have sufficient meat to keep the tribe alive. From Teba's thoughts, Billy learned that Bant was well recognized to be one of the tribe's better hunters. An injury to Bant *could* actually threaten the lives of everyone in the tribe.

Billy felt certain that his modern knowledge would make Billy/Teba a much better hunter than Bant had ever been. Bant would soon be superfluous. Billy made an effort to project this conviction to Teba. She remained absolutely unconvinced.

After pondering a moment, Billy decided to look for materials to "invent" a weapon. Whether such a weapon was used to injure Bant or instead used to teach the tribe a better way of hunting mattered little at this point.

First he went over to the area of the cave where the tribe's hunters made their weapons. There were quite a few spears lying about in various stages of creation or disrepair. Billy also found a good deal of fragmented stone and rock of various types lying around. As Billy/Teba found out by stepping on them, some of the fragments were quite sharp. However, Teba's feet were callused enough that sharp points which would have lacerated Billy's feet only felt uncomfortable to her. Billy wondered if any of the rock fragments were flint. He stirred through some of the small sharp flakes of stone, then picked up two of the larger ones and struck them together. A small amount of rock dust appeared at the impact site, but neither rock broke. Billy struck them together harder. This time one broke into multiple small fragments. Many of those small fragments had sharp edges on them somewhere, but none of them looked particularly useful to Billy.

Teba was horrified that he/she was even *touching* the men's equipment. When Billy looked up he saw the rest of the women staring aghast as well.

Billy banged the rocks together again. He tried striking them together at an angle. Most times he only created rock dust at the impact points; a few times he knocked off some larger pieces. *None* of the pieces seemed to have useful shapes. Billy shook his head, deciding that working rock or flint might take a lot more practice than he had expected. As he contemplated the mess he had made, he considered a vague memory that working flint had been a skill bordering on an art.

If that were true, then this did not appear to be where he was going to make a major change in the life of the cave.

Billy/Teba stood and turned to go back the other way. With some surprise he realized that everyone in the cave still couldn't believe what he'd been doing.

Teba's son Gano looked terribly dismayed. Although Billy himself didn't really care what Gano thought, he found Teba's emotions of embarrassment and dismay washing over him in uncomfortable waves. Without thinking he found himself practically rushing out of the men's area of the cave. Teba sheepishly wanted to explain what Billy/Teba had been doing there.

However she didn't really understand what the rock banging had been all about herself.

Billy, on the other hand, didn't feel that he needed or even *wanted* to explain himself to a bunch of ignorant cave people.

Billy thought for a moment, then decided to begin looking for supplies to build a fire. Billy considered what he knew about fire making. He knew that for one of the best known methods you took a straight stick and spun it between your palms, heating the tip by friction against a softer piece of wood. You could also use a bow, but that would require string and a piece of springy wood. He looked about the cave for a short straight stick which might be suitable. None were readily evident. He thought you needed a flat piece with a notch or pit in it for the straight stick to be drilled into. He didn't see any pieces of wood in the cave that appeared suitable. For a minute Billy was confused, thinking that the tribe must keep firewood somewhere. After a moment's delving into Teba's memory, he realized that since they hadn't had a fire for a long time they had little reason to stock firewood. The firewood they'd stocked had been used up for this or that project in the months since the fire had burned out. Following her thoughts, he went over to the wall where they'd kept wood in the past, but only found some scattered pieces, some of it full of dry rot. Billy/Teba left the cave looking for fire supplies. It was a beautiful day outside with the sky a pale shade of blue. There weren't any clouds. Some spots of snow that remained on the ground reflected light, making it very bright. Billy wished he had his sunglasses.

The air was briskly cool though only vaguely stirred by wispy little breezes. The cave was in the wall of a high embankment overlooking a small river which was running fast with muddy snow runoff. Evergreens were scattered about, as well as many deciduous trees which were just beginning to bud new leaves. Billy wondered if he could teach the tribe to fish in the river. He ransacked Teba's memories for fishing lore and found no recollection that she'd ever even eaten a fish.

175

He/she started down the trail toward the river. As they wandered about, Billy began to realize that nature supplied little in the way of straight sticks, at least in the area about the cave. In addition it appeared that almost everything was wet from the snowmelt. After some searching he/she found some small trees just sprouted and only a few feet tall. They had trunks which seemed fairly straight and only about as big around as his finger. They looked like they might be about right for a fire-drill. He grabbed one and tried to bend it sharply at the base in order to break it off. To his chagrin, it had an extremely tough springy trunk which he couldn't even come close to breaking.

Teba didn't have a knife, but did have a small hand-axe that she mostly used for scraping. Billy/Teba got out the stone and started hacking at the base of the little tree. His/her hacking scraped away bark and fibrous strands of the small tree's trunk, but more shredded than cut. After a moment of reflection, Billy realized that the stick he was producing would have a soft paintbrush like end which wouldn't be suitable for starting a fire anyway. In addition, he realized that the green wood contained in the stick wouldn't be dry enough for fire starting for weeks or months. With a grunt he/she set out to find something better.

Billy/Teba continued walking slowly along the path. Billy thought to himself that he should be enjoying the beautiful day. The rotten tooth aching in his jaw interfered with his enjoyment, to say nothing of the gnawing hunger in his stomach. He/she looked about hoping to see a rabbit or other animal which might make a meal, but as Billy contemplated this he realized that he/she had little hope of killing a rabbit with the tools at hand.

He/she picked up some stones to throw, but after a few practice throws, Billy got even more frustrated. Teba had never thrown a stone before and Billy's motor memories for throwing didn't seem to work well with Teba's smaller female body habitus. Generally the stones struck pretty wide of the mark, but Billy resolved to keep throwing for the practice. The skittering stones were surely driving away any potential prey, but it didn't seem like finding game would be useful until he/she had a *chance* of hitting something.

As he/she walked along, Teba became more and more frightened and the nervousness she felt imparted itself to Billy. As he contemplated his/her stressed mood, he realized that Teba's fears stemmed from being alone in the wilderness. Rummaging through her memories he realized that she'd seldom gone *anywhere* alone. In general, the women traveled in groups and, even then, they preferred to have a man with them for protection. For a moment, he gave her free reign to control their body. She immediately began turning her head about, looking for the large predator she felt sure must be creeping up on them.

Realizing with some chagrin that humans of this day and age really did need to fear large predators, Billy decided that he needed at least some kind of spear or club with which he could defend himself. To his intense frustration, even finding something as simple as a staff turned out to be more difficult than expected. He'd visualized a sturdy pole about six feet or so in length and an inch or inch and a half in diameter, but nothing even close could be seen in the surrounding area.

Cresting a small rise he saw some new growth trees to the left and made his way that direction. After looking for a bit, he found some small saplings which were close to what he'd been thinking of.

Then Billy/Teba was confronted with the difficulty of cutting one of *them* down with Teba's small hand axe…

Billy sagged back against the bole of a small tree and tried not to sob. Teba definitely wanted to cry. She couldn't understand why Billy was wasting time when they could be looking for food. To say nothing of straying far from the tribe where one of the big cats could make a meal of her. Cutting down the sapling with her little hand-axe had taken hundreds of blows. Surprisingly, it hadn't been as difficult as the attempt to cut the fire drill even though its trunk was bigger. The stem of the springy little tree he'd chosen for a fire drill had bounced the hand-axe away, whereas the hand-axe did cut into this bigger, stiffer shaft. However, Teba'd never tried to cut more than twigs with her hand-axe. Only after he'd started on it had Billy realized he himself had never cut any wood with an edged tool. He'd seen axes, hatchets, and machetes used in movies and, from that, he felt like he knew how. Now he realized that even if he'd had a better tool than the hand axe, it would have been more work than he'd expected. Teba's little hand-axe had a sharp edge, but it was small and required scores of accurate chops to produce a deep cut. Billy/Teba's accuracy was poor and his/her fingers were bruised where they'd smashed against the sapling trying to cut in at an angle.
The painful fingers put a damper on Billy/Teba's spirit too.
Once they'd gotten their emotions back in control, Billy started cutting the small branches off his new staff. Rather than cutting through the staff about six feet up as he had initially envisioned, he went to where it was quite small near the top and started scraping it to a point. In his mind he started calling it a "spear" instead of a staff. It was certainly easier to

scrape the small end of it down to a point than it would have been to cut through it a ways farther back. Billy/Teba stood back up and put the hand-axe into the pouch at Teba's waist. Billy had them practice lunging out to make stabbing motions with the pointed end, then swung the butt end to strike the trunks of several trees as if he were fighting with a staff. Feeling a little better about their safety, Billy started them back on their way.

The difficult project completed, their empty stomach started Billy thinking about food again.

Billy surveyed the landscape around him, thinking to see a rabbit or maybe even a deer. With nothing evident, he/she started walking. Billy swept the surrounding landscape with his eyes, hoping to see some prey animal. As they stepped around a rocky outcrop, Teba pulled their eyes to a fallen and moldering tree. Thinking that she might expect a rabbit or some other small animal to be hiding behind it, Billy turned that way, holding their spear at the ready. When they got to it, there were no animals present.

Billy felt frustrated, then realized that Teba wanted him to roll the rotting trunk over. Trying to hold his spear ready in case a rabbit burst out from under the tree, Billy put Teba's foot on the trunk and gave it a shove.

The fallen tree rolled part way, then broke apart. No rabbit. Just a disgusting mess of insects and worms.

To Billy's horror, Teba strongly wanted to reach out, pluck up, and eat some of the crawlers that looked like termites. She especially wanted to eat the mealworms. Saliva rushed into his/her mouth with anticipation of the crunch a few of her particular favorites would produce as she bit into them.

Teba started to crouch and her hand began to dart out toward a large bug she really wanted. Billy jerked it back, stood them back up and stepped away.

Billy wanted to heave.

Teba wanted to cry.

He continued onward, trying to block out Teba's disturbing thoughts.

When a large bird burst out of the grasses about ten feet in front of Billy/Teba, buzzing away into the distance and scaring the crap out of him, Billy thought it was a fluke. Not more than 100 feet further on, a rabbit shot off to the side and skittered away. Billy threw his spear after its bobbing-darting tail, but didn't come within five feet.

Realizing just how weak his ability to detect game was, he trudged after the spear.

The point he had carefully scraped onto the tip of his spear had broken. *Now* he had the staff he'd originally set out to make, though it was a little long.

Hungry, tired, sore, and with his/her jaw aching, Billy's vision blurred with tears. Frustration made him want to scream.

At first he continued to ignore Teba's gradually increasing anxiety, but when it became a full-fledged panic, he finally took note. Re-opening what he was thinking of as the "bridge" between her mind and his, he listened to her thoughts.

His eyes jerked back to their trail.

Wolves!

There were five of them, large rangy animals. Heads down, they were trotting his/her way as they appeared to follow a scent trail. The one in front had just lifted his eyes to focus on Billy/Teba.

Billy only considered fighting them for a moment before Teba's terror washed over him and he turned to run. Rattled, he almost dropped his staff. Only a few steps into his flight, Teba's loosely restrained breasts began to flop painfully. He remembered reading once that wolves *thrived* on running down fleeing prey. *I'm doing exactly what they expect and hope for!*

He tried to *reason*, after all that was Homo sapiens' great advantage. *Climb!* he thought. *Wolves can't climb!* He scanned desperately for a tree that he/she might be able to climb.

*There!* He/she swerved toward a dead tree which had stark limbs spaced a foot or two apart.

A spike of fear from Teba warned him that one of the wolves had caught up.

Billy pivoted, swinging his staff behind him. It smacked the animal in the side rather than the head as he had hoped.

Nonetheless, the wolf spun away with a surprised yelp.

Reluctantly, Billy dropped the staff and leapt for a branch. At first he was relieved that Teba's body had jumped high enough to reach it, then he felt consternation. Her arms were weaker than the arms he'd known as a man. They lifted him in a pull-up motion, which he suddenly realized meant they were relatively stronger than the arms of many women he'd known. However, he couldn't let go with one hand to grab at another limb.

As he dithered, Teba took over, throwing her legs around the trunk of the tree. They got a good grip and now he/she was able to switch one, then the other hand to the next higher limb. He/she surged up upwards, and reached for the next one.

Billy had already begun wondering how long they would have to huddle in the tree before the wolves would give up and leave.

Then a limb broke, and Billy/Teba fell.

Billy feared a broken leg, then death at the slashing teeth of the wolf pack, but Teba landed him/her like a cat, crouched, just in front of two startled wolves.

In horror, Billy looked for the staff. His eyes found it lying beneath the two wolves. Three more wolves were approaching.

Suddenly, he realized that he still had the broken tree limb in his hand. It had a satisfying heft, like a lightweight baseball bat. Gripping it like a bat, he swung it back like one.

The wolves, having lurched away when Billy/Teba suddenly landed almost on top of them, now bared their teeth and started forward.

Billy swung his bat like his team needed a home run. That swing felt better than any other in his life. Better than any homer he'd hit as a young man. The wolf saw it coming, but having had no experience with clubs, only began to draw away in the last few microseconds. The club smashed into its head, flipping the wolf end for end.

Billy tried to hit the second wolf on his return swing, but missed. It dodged back, then darted forward toward Billy/Teba's shins.

Billy swung again.

This time he connected with the wolf's shoulder as Billy tried to get his/her own legs away from the wolf's muzzle. The wolf went down with a squealing yelp.

Billy looked up at the other three wolves. They'd stopped and were eyeing him warily. He looked down at the two he'd hit with his bat. The head of the first one he'd hit was deformed. It quivered in what looked like death throes.

The other one backed away on three legs, then turned to guardedly eye its three compatriots. It limped slowly away and Billy watched with mixed horror and fascination as the remaining three healthy wolves eyed him for a minute, then turned to follow their injured pack mate. Their heads were low like they'd been when they were tracking Billy/Teba. Billy didn't have the feeling that they were preparing to offer their injured pack mate support.

They looked like they saw their next meal.

Billy stood uncertainly for a while, worried about whether the four wolves might return.
When they'd disappeared out of view, he looked around and began to worry a little about whether he could find the cave and the tribe again. Then he wondered if he wanted to? Billy really didn't like Bant. Teba's thoughts were bubbling, but Billy wasn't very interested. He picked up his staff and the broken limb which had actually saved him, then turned to start back the way he'd come.
Now, Teba's thoughts *exploded* completely through into the forefront of his mind. Her consternation that he was leaving the dead wolf behind shattered his other thoughts. Their hunger surged back into his consciousness from where it had been submerged by his/her fight or flight reaction to the wolves. He realized with some surprise that he'd let his modern revulsion against eating carnivores stand between himself and a meal.
Billy/Teba crouched, heaved the dead wolf over their shoulders and picked up their staff and club again. The wolf had to weigh close to 100 pounds, but Teba seemed undaunted. She'd carried heavy loads before.
Teba started off with a purpose. Billy, who'd been dominating their partnership most of the time, receded into the background. He wanted to think. With all the knowledge he'd brought from the future, they should be King/Queen here. He only needed to figure out how to introduce some new weapon or technology for everyone in this primitive world to recognize him/her as their leader. The question was, *which* technology to introduce.
Right now, the one he wanted to introduce the most was toilet paper! Even though Teba hadn't had a real meal for a couple of days, she still defecated. Then

183

she'd wiped herself with her own hand, wiping the hand clean on a handy rock. He'd been horrified by her first wipe, immediately stopping her hand from returning to her butt. He'd looked around for something to wipe with, finding nothing that looked suitable. Finally he settled for a handful of leaves from a nearby bush. To his dismay, their waxy surfaces did little to clean him. Staying in a squatting position he/she'd duck-walked around until they found some other leaves. Those cleaned better, but were painfully abrasive.

He'd been left feeling unclean and itchy until he'd found some moss a little further on and used it to clean him/herself. Teba, he realized, had none of the modern person's revulsion toward fecal matter so didn't mind getting it on her fingers. She only wanted to be clean because otherwise she itched. When he searched her mind for better solutions he realized that, when she could, she defecated near a stream and washed herself in it. This despite the freezing temperature of the water at this time of year.

Now Billy idly considered what he knew about paper making. It involved pulping wood somehow, he suspected with powerful machines. He knew that strong chemicals were involved, but had no idea which ones.

He snorted to himself, making paper was far beyond his knowledge base and wouldn't make him king anyway. What he needed to make was a *weapon*.

In times of yore, swords had made men into kings. Back when he'd been a modern man in modern times, Billy had thought a sword to be a simple weapon. Now, Billy realized that a sword was as far beyond him as a starship. He searched Teba's mind and found no recollection of anything that seemed like a metal of any type.

He knew that copper was one of the first metals to be used. Copper and gold could both be found in relatively pure form out in nature, but only in small quantities. For that matter, meteorites made of relatively pure nickel-iron could be found and were known to have been sources of iron in prehistory. But Billy wasn't likely to find a metallic meteorite. Gold was pretty, but didn't hold much of an edge. Even copper, if Billy could find it, wouldn't make a great sword. He was pretty sure that copper ores were frequently greenish or bluish. He supposed that if he found rocks those colors, he could try heating them in the hopes of extracting copper, but he feared that the heat required was more than could be achieved with burning wood.

Bronze was an alloy of copper, but Billy wasn't sure what the other metal was. He thought it might be tin, but it really didn't matter, he had *no* idea how to find tin.

Billy'd be better off looking for iron ore. He felt pretty sure that at least some iron ores were reddish in color. However, he thought the heat required to smelt iron was much higher than the heat for smelting copper. Having watched a video once on the making of katanas, he knew that air needed to be forced through the fire and the iron ore to provide extra oxygen. He thought they burned charcoal to produce the heat although he'd always found it puzzling that the charcoal remaining after a wood fire could still be burned and would produce more heat than the wood fire itself.

Still, though Billy knew something about extracting metals from the earth, and even though he suspected it was a lot more than most people, even in his home time knew, he was coming to the realization that he knew far too little. The knowledge of metallurgy that he did have, with years to experiment, would probably put him far ahead of anyone alive in this time, but it wouldn't help him *now*.

185

*God damn Kim anyway!* Billy didn't want to be here. He didn't want to be hungry. He didn't want to have this aching tooth. He didn't want to be scared and he didn't want to worry about what was going to happen when he ran into Bant again!

Billy didn't want to be a woman! Not in this day and age anyway He thought he wouldn't mind living as a woman in modern times, but in prehistoric times, when might made right, he didn't want to be a woman. He wanted some toilet paper… And a warm shower… And a beer…

Billy took a moment to peer out at the landscape through Teba's eyes. Teba had control of their body and he was riding along as if she were his autopilot. It was like when he got in his car thinking deeply about something else, then found himself driving into his own driveway a little while later without remembering the intervening trip. Billy wasn't quite sure where they were going, but decided it didn't really matter. As long as Teba was running their body, Billy could keep contemplating possible technological advances.

A bow and arrow seemed an obvious choice. He would need some kind of springy wood. He knew that yew wood had been considered the best for bows back before the availability of glues that allowed the layering of different woods. He thought it was something to do with yew already having layers of wood in it that had different properties. However, Billy had no idea what a yew tree looked like. What he needed was some ordinary kind of springy wood. Bamboo would be great and Billy knew bows could be made out of it, but he thought he was in Europe somewhere. The people in the cave had all had pale skin and if he were truly somewhere in prehistory, he thought that Europe was the only place pale skinned people could be found back then. Billy felt pretty sure that bamboo didn't grow in Europe until modern man transplanted it there.

Billy opened his connection to Teba's mind to see if she knew of a springy wood. To his frustration, the springiness of wood seemed to be something Teba had little or no interest in.

Giving up for the moment on wood for the bow, he pictured a string, thinking that surely Teba used string of some kind to bind things together. In fact... he looked at the furs she had draped about her body and saw that they had been roughly sewn together with some kind of heavy thread.

When he searched Teba's mind to learn about that thread, he found that it consisted of strips of fiber pulled off of animal tendons. She would use flakes of sharp rock to cut the fine strands that bound the tendon together. It would be easy to strip out thicker pieces of tendon, but getting one more than twelve inches long would be problematic. When Teba wanted something longer than twelve inches, she tied pieces of tendon together. Billy's exasperation surged. He didn't think that short pieces of tendon, tied together, would make a decent bowstring.

He couldn't believe it could be this hard!

Billy's whole life, being kind of a technical guy, he'd assumed that the knowledge he had of how modern things worked would put him head and shoulders above anyone even a few decades back. Now the old saying about "standing on the shoulders of giants" rattled through his mind. He'd never considered just how complex even the simplest things he took for granted actually were. He knew how a wheel worked, but even if he had a use for one right now, he realized that it could take him weeks to make one with no better tools than Teba's small hand axe. *You need tools, to make tools, to make tools...*

"Standing on the shoulders of giants" usually referred to the scientific knowledge passed on by those proverbial giants. He'd never given thought to the fact that the modern manufacturing of even a simple

187

object like a knife required first a miner who knew where iron ore was to be found and how to get it out of the ground. Then it required someone with the knowledge and equipment to smelt that ore and remove the iron from it. Next you needed people and furnaces and alloying materials to convert that iron into steel. Once you had the steel, ideally it needed to be worked to strengthen it, then shaped. Even if you had a piece of steel of the correct size and shape and all you wanted to do was put an edge on it, you would need the proper abrasives to do so and if you didn't want it to be *extremely* labor-intensive you would want those abrasives mounted on a powered wheel!

He realized that, starting from scratch, he didn't even know how to make good strong *string* for the bow he'd thought he'd invent. He thought, *I don't even have a* midget *to stand on!*

Billy'd been trying to think of an even simpler technology that he could invent in order to impress Teba's tribesmen when he realized they were arriving back at her cave.

He hadn't been paying much attention, but now observed that it was late afternoon. Although Teba had stopped to drink water at a couple of streams, she was gnawingly hungry. She was fervently looking forward to eating some of the wolf slung around her shoulders.

When Billy wondered why she hadn't eaten some of the wolf already, the knowledge flooded into his consciousness from hers. The women of the tribe were expected to share *any* food they obtained with the tribe. The men generally shared whatever they got on the hunt, but not always. No one would be surprised if the hunters brought down some small game like a ptarmigan and consumed it in the field without bringing any of it to the rest of the tribe. They thought of this as their right as hunters.

On the other hand, a woman who ate some of the food she gathered before she shared it with the tribe could expect a beating at the very least. Teba might have gotten away with eating a couple of mealworms from under that tree, out there far from anyone else, but she would have been *expected* to bring them all back and share them.

Billy, who'd never thought of himself as particularly socially aware, felt appalled. Not only that the men would treat the women in such a fashion, but that the women would stand for it.

Teba reacted to his rebellious thoughts as if they were ridiculously naïve. She considered it simply asinine to think that she or any other woman could revolt against the men of her tribe and survive. As if Billy's recollection of his/her casually brutal rape at the hands of Bant that morning weren't enough, her memories began to flash up other events from her relatively short life. Beatings, bullying, rape, casual killing.

The strong *ruled* the weak in this ferocious world and those who were the strongest ruled everyone else. The men were almost all stronger than any of the women and they ruthlessly took advantage of it! When Billy briefly considered the possibility that he/she should strike out on their own, leaving the tribe, Teba's mind considered it impossible. First, they would have to leave her son Gano, something she could never do. Second, though they'd been lucky enough to kill a wolf today, and Teba knew she could gather some food, she felt sure they'd soon be starving without the rest of the tribe. And then there was the fear. Not just fear of the large predators that populated the landscape, but fear of the men in her own tribe who would track her down.

And if those men didn't find her, the men of another tribe would.

189

Certainly no authority figure existed. No one who might punish the ruthless, cruel, vicious, and inhumane individuals of this pitiless society. Murder and rape were everyday facts of life, not occasional horrific occurrences that made the news. Billy considered himself to be a person who would stand up for the weak and downtrodden, but finding *himself* to be someone relatively frail shocked him. Even as he *considered* fighting back, memories of what had happened to him when he fought back against Bant surged back into the forefront of his consciousness. In dismay, he retreated from the forefront of their mind to let Teba handle their return to the tribe.

Teba slipped Billy's staff and club under the bushes about thirty feet short of the cave. Turning the corner into their area, she saw that the entire tribe was there. Eleven adults, of which six were women, plus three children. They'd started the winter with three babes as well, but, because hunting had been poor, none had survived.

She strove for an intermediate demeanor. She didn't want to appear cocky or the men would become angry, but she didn't want to appear cringing or they would take advantage of her. A quick glance around showed no evidence the men had had a successful hunt.

Her heart leapt with the knowledge that the wolf she'd brought would be *greatly* appreciated. Selah, Bant and Gano were the only ones who looked up as she approached. All of them had wide eyes.

If one of the men had brought in a kill by himself, the tribe would have had to listen to him bragging. Teba stepped to the center of the group, slipped the wolf from around her shoulder and laid it quietly on the ground in front of Selah. "A wolf pack attacked me. I killed this one," she said simply.

By then, *everyone* was staring. Teba could sense their joy as they anticipated full bellies. A glance under lowered brows showed consternation among the men that a woman had hunted successfully. And killed a *carnivore*! But for now, everyone waited in anticipation as Selah began deftly skinning and disjointing the wolf. Of course, she handed out the choicest bits to the men. They always got the choicest bits, claiming it as the hunters' right for bringing it in. Billy considered the irony of Teba settling for a tough, bony shank when *she'd* been the one to bring in the food. However, Teba was just happy that the men weren't being assholes. He felt revulsion as Teba began tearing into the raw meat, but the joy expressed by her body over the food it represented quickly overcame his distaste. With a shudder, he wondered, *Am I going to get so hungry I like eating bugs?*

Selah laid out the liver and quickly cut it into small pieces, one for each of the members of the tribe. She murmured something over it, then handed the pieces out with a reverent attitude. Having always hated even the smell of cooking liver, Billy expected at least the children to reject it, but everyone consumed their piece with evidence of great pleasure. The same held true for other internal organs, heart, lung, kidney, brain. Teba consumed her portions with relish while Billy tried to think of something else.

An older child was given the intestine to squeeze out and wash in the stream. Then, to Billy's dismay, they ate that raw as well.

Only after eating much more than Billy ever ate at one sitting, did Teba become full. But she kept eating, stuffing herself painfully. Billy worked some sums in his head, realizing that if the hundred pound wolf contained seventy pounds of edible material and you divided that among fourteen people it would average out to five pounds each! He knew from watching eating contests on ESPN that some competitive eaters ate substantially more than that at one sitting, but he'd once tried to eat a twenty ounce steak and hadn't even come close to finishing it.

As everyone, even the children, ate far more than Billy could believe, he realized that, with no refrigeration, this was how they stored their food. In their body's fat.

With a glance around, though their bodies were covered by furs, he saw in their bony faces that none of them had much body fat at the end of winter. Nonetheless, even after stuffing themselves with more than he could really believe, there was still some of the wolf left. Selah gathered it up and took it to the back of the cave. When Billy wondered why, Teba's thoughts made it clear to him that having it far away from them preserved it by keeping it cold during nights like they'd been having. When he wondered why they didn't keep it even cooler by putting it outside the cave her thoughts turned incredulously to all the small scavengers that would carry it away. Thinking about this, Teba worried that she and Gano would wind up on the outside of the tribe's huddle that night, a cold location. She hoped that having brought the food would gain her a good position near the warmer middle, but worried that having Bant angry at her would force her to the periphery.

As Teba worried about the cold, Billy started thinking about fire again. He'd picked up from Teba's thoughts that one of the main reasons they'd struggled this winter and lost their babies was because their fire had burned out one night early in the season.

They guarded their fires with great care because fire was so important to them and it could be so hard to get another fire if it burned out. Their last fire had come from a wildfire. Barso had been injured when he ran close to get a fire-brand. Then, one morning, despite stirring more and more desperately through the coals of the fire from the night before, they hadn't been able to find an ember that could be blown back to life.

Sometimes you could trade with another tribe for a start of fire, but tribes were superstitious that they might lose their own fire. If they did trade a fire start, they often demanded an unreasonable price. Even what might be considered by both tribes to be a reasonable trading value could still be beyond a tribe's resources. They had tried to trade for a fire start with the Stillwater tribe, but didn't have anything that the Stillwaters considered valuable enough to trade for.

Billy became excited. *Fire* was a technology that didn't require much in the way of pre-existing technology. Sure matches, or a lighter, or even a flint and steel would be great, but, in theory, all he needed was some wood and some friction. He'd given up on it this morning when he couldn't find a dry straight piece of wood for a fire drill, but he/she was much more likely to start a fire than make a sword!

Teba wanted to stay near the middle of the tribe, the better to position herself for the sleeping huddle. It would also keep her in the tribe's mind as the one who'd brought food.

However, Billy made Teba get up and they walked to the end of the tribe's shallow cave where wood had been kept back in the days when the tribe had a fire. Squatting, Billy/Teba sorted through the few pieces of wood remaining. He didn't know all that much about fires but he knew he didn't want green wood. All this wood was deadfall and it had been dry long before the fire burned out early in the winter. Unfortunately, Billy still couldn't find a straight piece suitable for a spindle or fire drill. Teba's hands were calloused and, he thought, tough enough to roll a spindle between them, but he didn't have any sticks straight enough to serve.

193

Picking out the straightest of the small dry branches, he/she placed it against one of the logs and tried twiddling it between Teba's palms, thinking that he might be able to do it even if it wasn't completely straight. But it didn't spin well, and the end he/she'd placed against the log tended to skitter around under the influence of the bend as it twirled.

There was no way he/she'd generate enough heat to start a fire that way. Frustrated, he cast that stick aside and started looking through the wood some more.

The lack of a good straight stick ruled out a fire bow too, even if he'd had good string and springy wood to make a fire bow out of. One thing that made him happy, despite the lack of a piece of wood for the fire drill was a log that split in half from dry rot when he tried to turn it over. The bottom half had turned to soft punk which he could easily tear apart into shredded bits. He thought the ragged punk would readily catch on fire. Even better, the top split of it was in pretty good shape. It was firm wood, he didn't know what kind, but he could dig a fingernail into it so he didn't think it was a hardwood.

Billy/Teba picked through some of the small branches until he found one that seemed like it was harder than the split log. Experimentally, he/she rubbed its base on the split surface of the softer wood log, running it along the grain. After about ten passes he touched the end of the stick.

It felt pretty hot!

Though Billy couldn't actually have a conversation with Teba's part of their shared mind, he'd found that if he wondered about something that she should know, the answer would bubble to the surface. Now he wondered, *If we could start a fire, what would be the best way to present it to the tribe?*

Her initial reaction was that, of course they *couldn't* start a fire. When it became obvious from his thoughts that he intended to try to start a fire anyway, she very strongly hoped that he wouldn't try to do it in front of everyone. First of all, she didn't want him doing anything that looked crazy where everyone could see, because after this morning's incidents, they thought she was weird enough already. Second, if, against all odds, he *was* able to start a fire, she wanted the method to be his/her secret.

After giving this some thought, Billy knelt Teba with her back to the tribe. They placed the log with its split surface up and its far end jammed up against a notch in the rock wall. Teba's calloused knee settled onto the near end of the log to immobilize it. He/she tore off some of the punk and put it on the far end of the log. They scooped up a couple of handfuls of the leaf litter from the floor of the cave and put it nearby, as well as a couple more twigs and small sticks of old dry wood that looked like they would burn readily.

Finally, taking a deep breath, Billy/Teba started rubbing the end of the stick on the split surface of the log. Pushing it away and dragging it back, pistoning it back and forth rapidly while pressing it hard against the split log.

It made a little groove, and as a bonus piled up some little filaments of shredded wood at each end of the groove.

As she knelt, pumping the stick vigorously back and forth hard and eventually starting to get a little tired, her son Gano showed up next to her and said, "What're you doing?"

Billy would have said, "Starting a fire," but let Teba say, "Making something," instead. Feelings their arms starting to ache, Billy began to wonder whether this piston motion would produce enough heat. He desperately wanted to stop and feel how hot the end of the stick was getting, but feared that he'd never have the stamina to pump it like this a second time.

A small curl of smoke appeared at the end of the groove. Billy'd just been thinking of giving up, but Teba, now more excited than Billy could have imagined, found new life in her arms and continued pistoning the stick back and forth. To her horror, she heard Bant grunt behind her, "That jiggling looks *good*." Bant knelt behind her and started pulling at her furs.

Billy was infuriated, but Teba was transfixed by what was happening in front of her and perfectly willing to ignore what was happening behind. A small flame appeared in some of the little shavings the stick had lifted. Continuing to piston the stick back and forth with her right hand she pushed some of the punk onto the flame with her left.

The punk caught on fire!

She put the leaf litter on top of it too and more fire blossomed!

Gano shouted, "It's a fire!"

Bant, who till then had been completely oblivious to what Teba was *actually* doing, leaned over her shoulder and saw the small flame. "Fire!" he shouted, letting her furs drop back down.

Moments later the entire tribe had gathered around exclaiming excitedly. Selah, who'd managed the tribe's fires in the past, knelt next to Teba and tenderly helped her build it up with small sticks and a couple of small dry logs. She turned to the crowd around them and shouted joyously, "Get wood!"

The tribe scattered into the twilight surrounding the cave.

Billy felt pleased.

Teba, *far* beyond pleased, was practically ecstatic.

Selah gazed at the small flame with reverence. She turned to Teba and said, "Can you watch over this fire, carefully feeding it small pieces of wood, while I prepare our fire pit?"

Teba moved to the side of her small fire so that she could watch Selah prepare the fire pit. Other members of the tribe started arriving back with arms full of deadfall which they began to stack where wood had always been kept. They immediately went out for more, excitedly chattering as they did so. Teba realized with some awe that even the *men* were getting wood, something they'd always considered beneath them in the old days.

Billy focused on Selah who almost ceremoniously cleaned out the small depression surrounded by a row of rocks near the middle of their sheltering overhang. Once it had been cleaned to her satisfaction, she spent a minute or two waving her hands over it in a fashion clearly ceremonial. Billy thought she might be supplicating some kind of gods or spirits. Next she came over and very carefully selected a few little sticks. She took them back and laid them in the center of the fire pit so that they formed a small grid. She returned for some punk, twigs and a few leaves that went on top of the grid. Next she got some small sticks and propped them over the grid in the shape of a little pyre. Finally she built a teepee of small logs over the rest of her materials.

After a little more ceremonial hand-waving, Selah returned to Teba and, speaking in what seemed like a very formal fashion for such a primitive society, she gravely said, "Teba, may I take a torch from your fire to start a fire for the tribe?"

Teba sat up straighter, raising her head proudly, and replied, "Yes, you may."

Rather than picking up a burning piece of wood from Teba's fire as Billy had expected, Selah picked up one of the pieces of wood from the old woodpile that was about an inch in diameter. She held it against the rock wall of the cave and, picking up a rock, pounded the end of the piece of firewood until it was split and

197

brushy looking. She held this blossom of broken wood in the flames of Teba's little fire until it was burning well.

Chanting, Selah stood with the burning firebrand held horizontally. She watched it for a moment or two, tipping the burning end downward so that the flame tried to climb onto the rest of the stick. Then, as everyone in the cave watched with fervent anticipation, she walked slowly to the fire pit and knelt worshipfully before the stack of wood she'd prepared. Lowering the firebrand she carefully placed it against the punk underneath her teepee of wood.

Billy had the impression that everyone held their breath.

A few minutes later flames were rising from the kindling, up through her little pyre and into the teepee of small logs.

One of the men threw his head back and began ululating joyfully.

The rest of the tribe joined him and a moment later, Teba threw her head back and began howling herself.


Dark had fallen outside the cave. For months, the cold had been painful and dangerous, especially at night. Though, on this evening, the air was as cold as it had ever been, the heat from the fire made Teba think of it as brisk rather than dreadful.

Instead of huddling together, shivering and praying for the dawn, the tribe sat around the fire with full stomachs, telling tales, laughing, dancing, and expressing their joy at being warm. Billy hadn't experienced a night with the tribe before, but he knew from Teba's memories and reactions that Teba's fire had improved the life of their tribe *immensely*.

Even better, from Teba's viewpoint, members of the tribe came to personally *thank* her for the fire. To Billy's surprise, none of them asked *how* Teba had started the fire. He had the impression that many of

198

them thought Teba had witnessed a miracle occurring and knelt down to watch it happen, rather than considering that Teba might willfully have caused such a miracle to transpire.

Even though Teba's tribespeople didn't seem to consider it possible that Teba actually started the fire, they nonetheless expressed their gratitude to her, perhaps attributing the fire to her karma, or prayers, or luck, or something else. While Billy would have felt more satisfied to have the tribesmen understand that Billy/Teba actually *created* the fire, Teba was perfectly happy to have the fire attributed to her in any fashion.

Eventually, the tribe settled down to sleep. Selah assigned a rotating watch amongst the women of the cave to be sure the fire kept burning through the night.

No one wanted to wake in the morning with their fire gone once again.

Billy lay awake for a long time. He understood through Teba's memories that the people of the tribe typically awoke with the dawn and fell asleep when dark came again. Because, especially in winter, this meant many hours were spent in darkness *trying* to sleep, many of them woke up part way through the night. This frightening part of the night was spent listening fearfully to the denizens of darkness and imagining that horrible beasts prowled about.

However, Billy was used to staying up in the evenings. He would have been watching TV or going out to bars in the evening back home. This night, he lay thinking about what other ideas he might introduce to improve the life of the tribe. He knew that Teba and the other tribespeople were looking forward to breaking open the wolf's bones and sucking out the marrow in the morning. Then, now that they had fire, the bones would be heated in water to make a soup. Billy was hoping that if he/she twisted the bones until they broke, some of them might break in a spiral fashion to produce a sharp point.

Maybe he'd be able to jam that point on the end of the staff he'd cut earlier today, making a spear.

He thought, I need to do something about this damn tooth…

Maybe…

Billy woke the next morning in his own bed. Kim was gone. She'd left a note, "Not as easy as you thought, was it?"

Despite searching for her, or anyone who'd ever known or even seen her, Billy never managed to make contact with Kim again.

I said, "But you *did* find it easy, right?"

Billy blinked at me, a look of bewilderment on his face, "Weren't you *listening*?!"

"Yeah. You were only there for a day, and you fed the tribe 'til they were stuffed *and* brought them fire!"

He shook his head, "Those wolves came this close," he held his fingers up, an eighth of an inch apart, "to eating me!" He thumped his jaw, "That tooth that hurt? It probably had an abscess and could easily have killed me. All these things I thought I could introduce—from swords, to knives, to metallurgy and blacksmithing, to spears, atlatls, bows and arrows—I couldn't even *start*!"

I shrugged, "Yeah, but you taught them how to start fires! That had to be huge! Teba gained a lot of prestige from it, so you sure as *hell* made a big difference for her."

Billy shook his head back and forth for a moment, then eventually shrugged acceptance. "Yes, it *was* huge. And I still kind of believe that if I'd stayed there for months, I *could've* given them better spears and maybe a spear thrower of some kind." He got a distant look, "Maybe with *years* I could've figured out how to make a bow and arrow. Metal and swords though," he shook his head. "Maybe in a lifetime, if the tribe were willing to feed me while I piddled around trying to figure it out." He looked deep into my eyes, "But lives were short back then man! That bad tooth? I had other teeth in rough shape, they just weren't completely rotten like the molar that hurt so bad. The people in my tribe were *all* missing teeth here and there, so Teba wasn't particularly worse off than they were. Their skin was pockmarked and unhealthy looking. Several of them limped. If I understood their system right, Teba counted eighteen summers and thought she was *old*, because only three people in the tribe had lived to count twenty."

"Well," I said, "I *still* think you beat Kim at her little game. Introducing fire in just one day had to be huge."

"Yeah..." he trailed off a beatific expression on his face. "It was." Then he shook his head, "But it was nothing compared to what I *thought* I could do. And I am *so* grateful to be back here..."

He sat a moment, staring into space, looking... wistful. I couldn't get over how different he looked. A changed man, so to speak. After watching him for a minute I said, "So, what. You look like you've got more to say—or maybe some deep thoughts to relate? Maybe you want to go back there?"

He looked up at me with a startled expression, "*Hell no*, I don't want to go back there." He paused for a moment's thought, "But on the other hand I feel ashamed..."

He didn't say anything more for a bit, so I prompted, "Ashamed of what?"

He turned to look me in the eye. "Teba's still back there, hungry, downtrodden, getting raped by that asshole Bant. Her son Gano—who *I* love because Teba loved him—Bant hits him too. A lot. I didn't solve that problem," he shrugged, "maybe I made it worse." He looked off into the distance, "And I really don't know *how* I could have solved it. The guy's a monster by modern standards, someone who taught me just how much of a jerk guys have been down through history…" He looked away, then back at me, "And still are! I've been a manipulative bastard myself and it makes me… ashamed. And angry. I'm not as bad as Bant, but… still, I regret the way I've acted…" He glanced at me again and gave a little grin, "I *really* want to go back and give Bant a little attitude adjustment." He shook his head, "Actually, I *want* to go back and kill him, but the tribe really can't afford to lose him."

He snorted, "I'm not so good at these moral judgments…" He looked up at me, "But, by God, I'm gonna get better."

He stared off into space again for a bit, then concluded by saying, "And, if that's what Kim really wanted, then *she* won… didn't she?"

### The End

What if - you went back in time?
*Would* your modern knowledge really make you king of the hill? And even if it did, wouldn't you still wish you were back in modern times? Even those who we think are *poverty-stricken* here in the United States actually live *better* than the kings of yore (warmer housing; better, cleaner clothing; more varieties of food, with priceless spices easily obtained; flush toilets; heated water; bathing; telephones; televisions; music on demand; fast transportation; far less disease; and free basic education), but we seldom give it any thought.

Actually, most of the time, we just complain…

## GUITAR GIRL

Keith walked out onto the patio of the Piña Colada Bar where his band, The Sons of Beaches, had been gigging for the summer. Typical for this time of day, the patio was nearly empty. A young couple had their heads bent together over a big umbrella drink they were sharing with a pair of straws. Over to one side, a slender girl sprawled back in a chair that faced out toward the ocean. Her body looked cute, though Keith could only see it from behind. What caught his attention was the fact that she had an electric guitar in her lap. She plucked idly at the strings, eyes on the surf, listening to her instrument through a pair of earphones.

Giving her little thought, Keith busied himself uncovering their equipment and powering it up. His band had a little stage at one end of the big patio. By the end of a typical evening, they'd have a pretty good crowd. Some sitting at the bar near the back of the patio, some at the tables scattered around the patio and some out on the nearby beach. Early in the evening, they'd play mellow stuff for the people having dinner. Later, people would be dancing and the band would try to play stuff that fit whatever kind of crowd they had that night. They took pride in being able to play a wide variety of music and usually being able to find a groove that made the crowd happy. Dave showed up and checked on his drum kit. He took his cymbals home every night, so he had to set them back up. He settled onto the throne and ran through a very short drum solo that made sure everything sounded okay and confirmed that the kit was miked correctly. By then Bernie had arrived, tuned his bass guitar and jacked it into the sound system.

Satisfied, Bernie gave Keith a nod. Keith played a sustained D chord on the keys, bringing the volume up slowly with his pedal. Bernie bobbed his head a couple of times, then started thumping strings on the bass. Dave brought in a beat on the drums and a few seconds later, having finished the intro, Keith leaned forward and sang, "Nibblin' on sponge cake…"

As they worked their way through Margaritaville, Keith saw the girl reach up and pull out one of her earphones. It looked to him like she wondered what she was hearing. Earphone out, she turned to look back over her shoulder and saw the band. Curious as to how she would react, Keith kept an eye on her. The girl turned back to look out to sea, then looked down the beach to the right and the left. He got the impression that she was looking for some convenient quiet place to go, now that the band had taken over the patio. Evidently, she didn't see anything satisfactory, because she kind of shrugged then leaned her chair so that it rose onto one back leg. Shuffling her feet, she pivoted the chair on that single leg until she was facing the band. His eyes widened. He'd thought she might be cute when he'd seen her body from behind. Now he saw her from the front— the girl was hot!

She settled the chair, then adjusted her earphones. She reinserted the one she'd pulled out, but Keith thought she'd put it in loosely. She tugged on the other one, Keith suspected to loosen it as well. Fitting his impression that she'd loosened both earplugs so she could hear the band, she started playing the guitar again. She changed chords when the song changed, so Keith felt pretty certain that she was playing along with them.

At first, Keith felt surprised to see that she had the chord progression of Margaritaville down pat. Keith mostly played keyboards, but he also played guitar on a few songs. He'd certainly played enough that he could see that she was fingering the correct chords. She didn't hesitate as she played, or make sudden moves on the fretboard suggesting that she'd played something incorrectly, so, even though he couldn't *hear* what she was playing, he was pretty sure she was playing it well.

His surprise only grew as the band played song after song in a wide variety of genres and styles. Either she knew *every* one, or she faked it better than anyone he'd ever seen.

By the time they'd finished their first set, Keith's curiosity was overwhelming him. Their little band played a little something for everyone, new to old, classic rock, to pop, to country, to reggae, to hip-hop. After all, they were trying to keep a broad variety of customers happy, though he worried sometimes that it meant there was something in their set list for each customer to dislike as well. In any case, it seemed to him that it had to be *extremely* unlikely that anyone would know *all* the songs they'd played unless they'd had the set list and studied them.

He wondered if their little band might have just captured itself a groupie. Someone who'd listened to them many times before. It seemed highly unlikely that a good-looking young girl like this one could be interested in a three piece band made up of guys in their late thirties, but he could dream, couldn't he?

As they took their break, Keith wandered back to the bar where Nicole had his soda water and lime ready. Usually, he went back in the band's dressing room and checked email on his phone, but this time he wandered out to where the girl was sitting, wondering how to strike up a conversation. She'd turned back to face the surf and was staring out over the water, still idly playing her guitar.

Standing to the side and just barely closer to the beach, he turned and watched her out of the corner of his eye. The first thing that struck him as he saw her close-up was that she wasn't just pretty, like he'd thought.

The girl was stunning!

Trying not to stare like a creep, he focused his eyes on the guitar. He didn't recognize it. It didn't have a brand emblazoned on it and didn't look like any guitar he'd ever seen before. Nonetheless, everything about it seemed to be very well-made with excellent fit and finish. He was put off, though, by an extensive array of switches and knobs and buttons practically covering its body. His first impression was of a guitar made for some kind of technophile who couldn't really play. The kind who thought that if his instrument had enough fancy tone controls, it'd make up for a lack of talent.

Then Keith's eyes tracked to the fingers working the neck of her guitar because she'd just bent the strings like a blues guitarist. Then her fingers started flying around the fretboard like a classical guitarist. *It really looks like this girl can play!* However, he felt a little put off by the fact that she had a large ring on her ring finger. It was plain silver and covered much of the back of her finger. It didn't seem to get in the way of her playing very much, but he found it odd that a serious guitarist would wear such a large piece of jewelry on their playing hand.

Keith could faintly hear the notes on the unamplified electric guitar over the sound of the surf and the customers who'd started filling the patio bar, but what he heard sounded good. It wasn't a song he'd ever heard before, but he already liked it.

Wondering how to get her attention, he looked at her face and realized she was eyeing him. He gave her a little two-fingered wave.

She reached up and pulled out an earphone. "Hi. You play keyboards in the band, right?"

Keith nodded, then gave a little wave at the guitar, "You look like you play pretty well yourself. What kind of guitar is that?"

"I've got a friend who makes them."

Keith's experience with instruments made by guys in small shops was limited, but the ones he'd seen had been big on gee-whiz and low on actual sound quality. Still, it looked well-constructed, as if whoever'd made it was technically competent at least. Maybe her buddy really did turn out a decent instrument. "It looked like you were playing along with us in our first set. Did you really know *all* those songs?"

She shrugged and looked a little bit embarrassed, "Yeah, I know a *lot* of songs…" she shrugged, "all the songs you played anyway. I like to play along 'cause I think it's good practice. Besides, I like classic rock and you played a bunch of that."

Keith looked back over his shoulder. Dave and Bernie weren't back yet, but he didn't think they'd be upset about him inviting a girl this cute to play with them. Looking back at her with a shrug of his own, he said, "You want to join us on stage and play along on the next set?"

She frowned a moment as if giving it serious thought, then glanced at her watch, "I'm here on a family vacation and we're supposed to eat here on the patio in just a few more minutes." She looked back up at him, "How about the set after that one?"

Thinking about how disappointed he was going to be when her husband and kids showed up for dinner, Keith tried not to show it, saying, "That'd be cool. Just give me the high sign when you're ready to play and I'll invite you up to the stage. What's your name?"

"Eva," she said, glancing off to the side, then standing up without giving her last name. "My folks just came in, so I'll catch you a little later." She stood, slung her guitar over her back and walked away.

*Nice legs,* Keith thought as he admired her retreating form. Then he noticed Dave and Bernie staring at him from the stage.

When Keith stepped up on the stage Bernie rolled his eyes, "There was no way you had *any* chance with a girl that looks *that* good!"

Keith raised an eyebrow at his bandmates, "She's eatin' dinner with her family, then she's going to play a few songs with us on the set after this one."

Bernie snorted, "You got it bad, don'tcha! You know... just 'cause she *looks* good and carries a guitar, that doesn't mean she can play worth a damn."

Keith played the opening chords of "I Want to Know What Love Is" while he said quietly, "I'll bet she can."

Both Dave and Bernie rolled their eyes at that one. Dave said, "She's way too young for you anyway."

As they played the next set, Keith's eyes kept returning to the girl's table. She and her family had been seated at the edge of the patio, far from the band's little stage. As he'd hoped, her "folks" appeared to be her parents. There was a young man with them too, but Keith thought he looked younger than Eva. Hopefully he was her little brother. He chided himself, *Like Dave said, she's way too young for me. It might be interesting to have her play with us, but I've got to be realistic!*

By the time the Sons took their next break, Keith thought Eva and her family might be finishing up their dinner. This time he took his club soda and lime back to the dressing room with Dave and Bernie. Bernie lifted his chin at Keith and said, "What are you going to do when this girl stinks up the place?"

Keith frowned, "I was planning to give her a choice of several songs. I'm sure she'll pick one she knows pretty well."

"*Sure* she'll pick one she knows, but still, she's an *amateur*. Just because she knows a song doesn't mean she'll play worth a damn! *You're* the one who's dragging her up on the stage, you need to have a plan for how you're going to ease her off when she starts to embarrass us."

Irritated, Keith said, "Come on! I didn't just go ask her to play because she looks good and carries a guitar! I watched her during our first set, and I'm pretty sure she played the right chords to *every* song we played. And I watched her playing by herself during the break, she was bending the strings. If she's not any good, I'll kiss your asses!"

Dave turned his back and bent over, "You'd just as well kiss it now."

Keith pulled an ice cube out of his drink and dropped it into the back of Dave's pants while he was bent over. "You guys are a pair of crotchety old men," he said. Turning toward the door, he said, "I'm heading back out."

Keith got another club soda and lime and headed back up onto the stage. While he waited for the other guys he tuned his guitar since he hadn't played it during the first couple of sets. Surreptitiously, he sent his eyes around the patio, disappointed because he didn't see the girl.

When Dave and Bernie got out to the stage, Bernie nudged Keith and said, "Hah! She stood you up!" But, after they played their first song, Keith recognized the girl leaning on a post near the edge of the patio. She had a black baseball cap on backwards that covered her reddish blonde hair. A strap crossed her chest, so he was pretty sure her guitar hung behind her. Eyeing her, he lifted his eyebrows interrogatively and played a second or two of air guitar. She nodded. Keith leaned to the mike and said, "The Sons of Beaches would like to invite our new friend Eva up to play a song or two with us." He heard Bernie snort behind him as the girl leaned away from the post and started walking toward the stage. Bernie started playing the bass line from Blurred Lines. Dave started the beat on the cowbell and kick drum. Keith knew they were trying to embarrass the girl with the sexy/sexist song. He shot them a quick glare, but they pretended to be oblivious and kept it up. Rather than looking offended, Eva crossed the floor with a little strut that picked up the beat. Keith saw that strut drawing eyes from all around the bar.

Keith leaned down to give her a hand up onto the little stage. She took it graciously, though she obviously needed no help. She leaned close, "What channel?" He blinked, then realized she was asking about the UHF channel on their wireless musical instrument system. He'd been thinking that she would jack in with a cord and had laid one out for that purpose. He looked over at their wireless receiver, wondering if she had a transmitter since they didn't have an extra. He said, "Channel 6?" He looked back at her, "Ours is an AKG system, do you have a compatible transmitter? We don't have an extra." He looked at her again and realized that she didn't have an equipment bag and certainly didn't have room in the pocket of those snug shorts to be carrying a transmitter.

"Yeah, it's built in," she said, deftly twisting one of the many knobs on the body of her guitar. She flipped a few switches.

Keith said, "Do you know..." he broke off when the girl started strumming the guitar. His first thought was that she was embarrassing herself, him, and the band, by doing a sound check when the drums and bass were already playing something. Though, he thought, it served the guys right for playing a song that didn't really even have a guitar part when a guitarist was coming up to join them. Then, he realized as she faded in the volume that Blurred Lines *did* have a guitar part. The original version didn't have one and he'd never heard anyone play the song with a guitar part, but the girl was playing ringing, choppy little chords that fit right into it.

They sounded great!

Keith turned and lifted an eyebrow at Bernie whose eyes were wide with surprise.

Normally, Keith sang the song and the guys had cycled through the intro a couple of times by now so he turned toward the microphone. Before he got there, Eva stepped up to it, gave him a wink, and started singing:

"If you can't hear

What I'm tryin' to say…"

Robin Thicke's original version had been sung in a high-pitched falsetto. Eva imitated it flawlessly. Except, she sounded a lot better.

Keith looked out at the people in the bar. Crowds could be notoriously fickle. They were especially hard to please with popular songs that they expected to sound like the original versions. *He* liked Eva's choppy little chords, but worried that their audience wouldn't.

He needn't have worried, people were streaming out onto the dance floor, even though it was earlier than people usually danced at the Piña Colada Bar.

Keith refocused on their music. He really liked both Eva's chords and her vocals. He couldn't really put his finger on just what was so great about them, but *something* was. *This girl could make it big someday*, he thought to himself. He wondered what he should be doing. Eva was singing and there really wasn't a keyboard part for this song so he was somewhat at loose ends. Then she gave him the eye as it came time for Pharrell's and T.I.'s parts, and he sang those.

The song wound down, and Keith wanted to keep the crowd out on the dance floor. He turned to Eva, "You know, 'I Gotta Feeling'?"

She didn't answer, only gave him a sly grin as her fingers scampered over the switches and knobs on her guitar again. Then she started playing the intro chords for I Got a Feeling. Chords he usually played on his keyboard using what he thought was the same guitar patch the Black Eyed Peas had used.

Keith thought it sounded better played on her guitar. He began thinking that whoever had made an electric guitar with all those effects built right into the body must be a really talented dude. Keith started playing the synth strings and singing Will.i.am's part. He looked back out at the dance floor.

People were going crazy.

Eva sang Fergie's parts perfectly. Once again, he thought she sounded better than the original. As he watched the crowd, he thought they may be thinking the same thing.

When they finished "I Got a Feeling," he started to ask her if she knew "Love Shack," but she'd lifted an eyebrow. She'd already started picking the intro notes to "Sweet Home Alabama." The Sons had played that song in their first set, but it had been a soft version with Keith playing the lead on the keyboard. Eva played the lead with a slightly rougher, more distorted guitar tone than Lynyrd Skynyrd had used.

It sounded awesome! More and more people were crowding onto the dance floor and people were filtering into the bar from the beach. Keith wondered exactly what was happening. Sure, the girl sounded good, great even, but could it be such a big difference that it would draw a crowd like this? Or was something different going on?

They finished "Sweet Home Alabama" and she pulled a weirdly distorted, distant scream sound out of her guitar as she leaned to Keith and said, "You guys know 'Another Brick in the Wall'?" When he nodded, she started strumming the chords of the intro even as the scream slowly faded out. He started to glance back at Bernie, wondering if Bernie had picked up on what she was playing, but then he heard the bass come in right where it should. Her odd guitar now sounded just like David Gilmour's... except... somehow just a little better. As Keith started to sing, "We don't need no education..." He once again wondered how she was doing it. He didn't think of "Brick in the Wall" as a great dance song, but when he looked out at the floor it seemed to be even more crowded. Some were dancing, many were just swaying to the music, eyes focused on the stage. Eyes focused on Eva! He looked around. The whole damn bar was standing room only! There were people *up on chairs*!

Keith shook his head. He'd never seen *anything* like what was happening this night.

As they wound Brick down, Keith wondered how to keep this phenomenon going. Despite his gut, which said the crowd's unbelievable response was to Eva, he kept hoping that maybe his band had just finally found their groove and she was only a layer of icing. *Maybe we could invite her to join the band? A good looking girl guitarist might be what it takes for us to move to the next level!*

They'd just played two songs that he thought of as classic rock, so now Keith wanted to play something more current. Something that had a good guitar solo. He thought for a moment, then leaned to her as she faded her strumming away and said, "Do you know Eve of Destruction's 'High Burn'?" As soon as he said it, he regretted it. The song had a guitar solo all right. One that virtually *no one* could play. When the Sons played the song, they just skipped the section that had the guitar solo in it because there was no way they could do it justice. He couldn't play anything like it on the keyboard, and he sure as *hell* couldn't play the guitar that well.

But Eva just grinned and nodded, showing him a cute dimple he hadn't seen before. Hoping she could play something that wouldn't embarrass her, Keith turned to Bernie and mouthed "High Burn."

Bernie raised an eyebrow in some disbelief, but started drumming his fingers on the low bass string like the bassist from Eve of Destruction. He mouthed back, "*With* that solo?!"

Keith shrugged. Dave brought in a solid backbeat and Keith punched up the Hammond B3 patch on his synth and started filling in with low chords.

Eva's hand slid down the neck of the guitar, pulling out a rising, wailing, tone. The lead guitar part came to life. Keith blinked as he realized that she'd flipped over that oversized ring and was using it as a slide. *Maybe it's not such a ridiculous thing for a guitarist to wear after all.* He felt even more impressed with her custom guitar because whatever effects it contained, they were imitating the sound of the guitar on the original song by Eve of Destruction…

Which, he suddenly realized, was played by a girl.

A beautiful girl with black hair… named Eva!

Keith's eyes rose to focus on her face. *This* girl was strawberry blonde, but hair could be dyed. Right now, with the black baseball cap covering her hair, you wouldn't even know she was blond.

Eva from Eve of Destruction was supposed to be pretty reclusive, avoiding photos and staying out of the limelight. No one even knew her last name.

Certainly Keith hadn't seen any close-ups to know exactly what she looked like.

She gave him a knowingly delighted grin and started into the guitar solo.

The girl played that *astonishingly* complex solo.

The one that had stumped so many of the gods of guitar.

Keith would have sworn she played it perfectly, note for note. All the effect changes that he'd thought had probably been pre-recorded in a studio—those were made by touching switches or knobs on the body of that guitar with flying fingers.

Trying not to gape, Keith looked up at her grin, then out at the crowd.

He realized that the intermittent noise he'd been hearing came from all those people roaring "Eva... Eva... Eva..."

Somehow, as the song faded to a close, she'd managed to fade to the back of the stage.

By the time the last notes died away, she was gone. No one saw where she went.

Later, Keith would remember that night as magical. To himself, he would wonder with embarrassment how he could have invited one of the world's most famous musicians, someone who filled *stadiums* with adoring fans, up onto the stage of the Piña Colada Bar to play a set with the Sons of Beaches... and not even known who she was.

Most of the time, he didn't let on. When people asked him about it, he'd just frown and say, "Of course I knew..."

**The End**

Inspired by the urban myth that a vicar, not knowing who Eric Clapton was, but seeing that he owned several guitars, invited him to play at church—giving him several weeks to practice up before he did it.

215

*Hope you liked the book!*
*If so, please give it a positive review on Amazon.*

**Acknowledgements**

I would like to acknowledge the editing and advice of Nora Dahners, Gail Gilman, Elene Trull, Mike Alsobrook, Philip Lawrence, Kat Lind, and Abiola Streete, each of whom significantly improved these stories.

Made in the USA
Las Vegas, NV
16 March 2022

45739027R00125